REALM OF THE
GOLDEN DRAGON
A SEA STORY

C.D. Williams

For

Elena

Thanks for the great service

Pocol Press

Clifton, VA

Hope you like my story

BEST WISHES

C. D. Williams

POCOL PRESS
Published in the United States of America
by Pocol Press
6023 Pocol Drive
Clifton, VA 20124
www.pocolpress.com

Publisher's Cataloguing-in-Publication

Names: Williams, C.D.
Title: Realm of the golden dragon : a sea story / C.D. Williams.
Description: Clifton, Virginia : Pocol Press, 2016.
Identifiers: ISBN 978-1-929763-67-2 | LCCN 2016932577
Subjects: LCSH Vietnam War, 1961-1975--Fiction. | United States.
Coast Guard--History--Vietnam War, 1961-1975--Fiction. | War stories.
| Action and adventure stories. | BISAC FICTION / Action & Adventure
| FICTION / War and Military | FICTION / Historical.
Classification: LCC PS3623.I556465 R43 2016| DDC 813.6--dc23

Library of Congress Control Number: 2016932577

Cover and interior art by Larry Stoffregen.

Dedicated to my Shipmates
The men who sailed with me aboard
The U.S. Coast Guard Cutter *Basswood* W388
From October 1966 to October 1968

A SHIP

A ship is just a ship without her crew. It's the crew who breathes life into a mindless, floating conglomeration of steel and machinery. It's the crew who lovingly cares for her and sails her across the seas. It's the crew that makes a ship all that she is capable of being.

So, what is a ship? To those who sail in her she is a home, an occupation, a source of pride, and a source of adventure. She is a fickle lady who's tossing and turning on an angry sea can threaten your very life, but to know her is to know your first love. She provides you with comrades and camaraderie, a warm bunk, and travel to exotic places. She also provides you with sights and sounds and smells you will experience no other place.

No matter what you do with the rest of your life, you will never forget her or the seas you sailed together.

C.D. Williams
Chief Warrant Officer
U.S. Coast Guard, Retired

ACKNOWLEDGEMENTS

First of all I would like to thank my wife Maripi for a lifetime of loving support.

My everlasting thanks goes to the U.S. Coast Guard for sending me to the many diverse and exciting locations that I have written about in this book.

I would like once again to thank Mr. Robert Cawley, Hollywood screen writer and novelist and my writing instructor at the College of Southern Nevada. His guidance helped stoke the fire to write in my belly.

I am also forever grateful to my old *Basswood* shipmate Larry Stoffregen for his wonderful artwork in creating the cover for this book.

My thanks also go to Mr. J. Thomas Hetrick, my publisher, for taking a chance on this new and unknown writer.

Last but not least. Please allow me to acknowledge the memory of Gunner's Mate First Class Daryl Carlson. My shipmate, my friend, my mentor, and my tour guide to the mysteries of Asia and the Far East. Rest in peace, Guns.

AUTHOR'S NOTE

This is a somewhat irreverent tale of life aboard a small Coast Guard ship deployed to the far reaches of the Western Pacific and other Asian seas. Welcome aboard.

I've been kicking this story around for a lot of years. It started out as a memoir of my six most exciting years in the Coast Guard. I have decided, instead, to write two of those years as a historical novel.

The ship in this story was real as were the times and locations. In the 'truth is stranger than fiction' category, many of the incidents in this novel have been described more or less as they actually happened. All names have been changed to protect the innocent as well as the guilty. My old *Basswood* shipmates may recognize some of the characters in this novel and I use the term 'characters' advisedly.

Novel my ass, any old sailor who gets his hands on a copy of this book will instantly recognize it for what it is. A damned straight, "this ain't no shit," sea story. So, what is a sea story, you may ask?

Sea stories are often humorous, and may be based on a real event or events.

With time, many retellings, the vagaries of memory and the stylized humor of the story teller, a sea story often becomes a highly embellished version of reality. Sea stories are often told while on liberty or shore leave. The venue is usually a sailor bar and they always start "This ain't no shit."

A few (okay many) embellishments to real incidents have been made and some purely fictional scenes added. Some time sequences have been altered to improve the story line and readability, to add continuity and to hold the reader's attention. My readers will decide if I've succeeded.

The *Basswood* actually was in Vietnam in 1967. We worked in the rivers and bays all up and down the coast and we did have Navy SEALS on board during part of our time there. However, the joint operations with the SEALS and the combat action segments described in the book are all fictional and a product of the writer's imagination. They were added to give the boys on the *Basswood* a few tense moments.

I've sailed to and have visited all the places that I've written about in this book. I hope that I have faithfully described these times and places. Enjoy the trip.

ABOUT THE TITLE

Crossing the 180th Meridian, a.k.a the International Date Line, on a military ship is accompanied by a time honored initiation ritual. Upon completion of the initiation, sailors become card carrying Golden Dragons. This then is their admission to the mysteries and adventures to be found in Asia and the Far East. This novel follows the crew of the U.S. Coast Guard Cutter *Basswood* on one such journey.

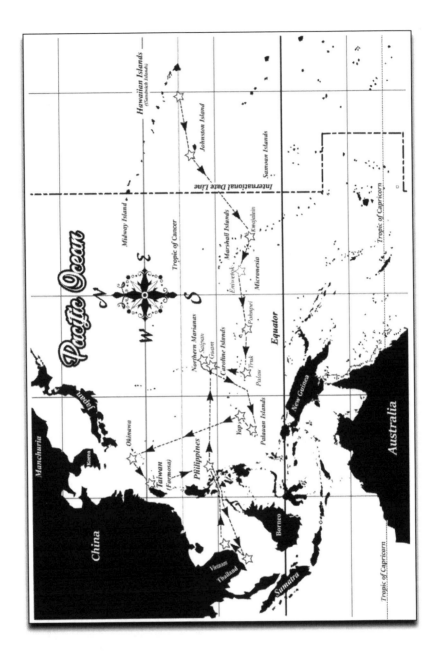

TABLE OF CONTENTS

PROLOGUE

It was an early evening in April 1968. Guns and I were sitting in our favorite corner of the Merchant Marine Club having a goodbye drink. "Born to be Wild" by Steppenwolf was playing on the jukebox and we were reminiscing about our past year and a half together on the Coast Guard Cutter *Basswood*. Guns was rotating back to the States in the morning, flying out of Anderson AFB on the other end of the island.

The Merchant Marine Club was located just a short walk from where our ship tied up in Apra Harbor on the island of Guam. The only other place nearby where you could get a drink was the big Navy Base EM Club, but who wants to drink with 500 noisy squids? No, the Merchie Club was fine with us. It was a rough and tumble place that resembled nothing so much as a Wild West saloon. The only people who patronized the bar were Merchant Marine sailors and a few Coasties. You would buy a bottle of the booze of your choice and nurse it until you were ready to leave. Guns and I were at our favorite table doing just that.

"Shit, Doc, it seems like only yesterday that you were coming up the brow in Hono and reporting for duty."

"Yeah, time flies when you're having fun Guns, and we've certainly been having fun. Well, except for our little dust up in Vietnam."

"No shit, who'd a thought a couple of old liberty hounds like you and me would get mixed up with the God-damned Navy SEALS. And getting our asses shot at no less."

"It's hard to get past losing Jackson Randy," I said. "That Alabama hick had a set of big ones on him the way he held off the VC with that damned old .50 caliber machine gun of yours."

"What about old Montana, going back and getting Jackson after he was hit?"

"Yeah, that was something. A silly millimeter more and the wound he got at the base of his neck could have been in his carotid artery or maybe his head," I responded.

"I hear that Navy SEAL officer is putting them both in for medals."

"Well, they both deserve them," I said. "I don't mind telling you my grommet was cinched pretty damned tight while all that lead was flying around, like scared shitless."

"You weren't alone my friend, you weren't alone," Guns responded.

"Okay, enough of the depressing stuff." I said. "Other than Vietnam, you've gotta admit it's been a hell of a tour. We've sailed all the way from Blue Hawaii across the wide-ass Pacific and most of the seas in Asia. You know Guns, I counted them up the other day. Including the Bird Watcher Patrol, we've been to forty-three different islands and five Asian countries, counting Vietnam."

"Yep," he responded, "and some of the best darn liberty ports in the world, most of them more than once. You'll pick up a few more islands on that medical research trip next month. I'm kind of glad I'll be gone, but it will be a good trip for a semi-egghead like you."

"Well, so far it's been a hell of a trip. Guns, do you realize that we'll probably never see another tour of duty like this?"

"Now that's a damned shame, but you're probably right. It was a once in a lifetime trip."

"Hey Doc, you remember when you first arrived in Honolulu, before I took you in hand and showed you the ropes?"

"Yeah, you sure straightened me out or I'd have been stroking it into my socks like the deck force kids down in the zoo (crew berthing). You told me 'Shipmate, you're wasting your time trying to pick up the tourist chicks down on Waikiki Beach. It's the sixties, you have short hair and you're in the service. You have to go native.'"

"Well, you were right, shipmate. I started frequenting the Japanese and Korean bars. I learned a little of the lingo, ate the food, and pretty soon I was getting more ass than a toilet seat. In this part of the world the word is "go native" and it has served me well every place we've been in the last year and a half. You've been a great tour guide shipmate, and I'm really going to miss your skinny ass."

"Not if you get the orders you requested to that 180 home ported in Sangley Point in the Philippines. The first night you hit the beach in Cavite City and hook up with one of them pretty little Filipina gals, you'll forget all about old Guns."

"No way man, I'd be wishing you were right there with me a Brave Bull in your hand (Guns' favorite drink) and your own girl sitting on your knee. It doesn't matter anyway. There's no way the medical brass are going to leave me out here for back-to-back tours.

They say it's not good for corpsmen because we tend to go wild, get too independent, and that makes us a little rough around the edges for civilized clinical duty in the States. And that's probably where I'll end up, in some damned outpatient clinic handing out band-aids and aspirins to desk sailors. So, what do you think about your orders?"

"Could be worse, I've been stationed in Boston before. It's a good sailor town and there are plenty of sailor bars down on the waterfront where my ship ties up. The ship is one of those new 378-foot cutters. If I'm lucky, she might pull a Cadet Cruise to Europe. I couldn't get in any more trouble there than I have here, probably less since you won't be there."

"That's probably true, speaking of trouble, do you remember when we took that .50 caliber machine gun you had just repaired over to Ft. Shafter Army Base to test fire it and ended up shooting up one of their field exercises? That seems funny now, but it was just a lucky break that we didn't kill any of those dog faces."

"Those Grunts didn't have a very good sense of humor did they? Shit, that was good live fire experience for them, helped make their training more realistic. At least that's the way I've always looked at it. How about when you got that albatross caught in your fishing line and killed it when we were on the Bird Watcher Patrol."

"Oh yeah, I was trolling off the fantail. We were making about 9 knots, good speed for trolling. That damned bird went for my lure and got tangled up in the stainless steel leader.

All the bird scientists were out on deck watching me fish. I'll never forget the horrified looks on their faces when I hauled that dead bird aboard."

"Well Doc, you can look at it this way, you disproved the old sailor myth that killing an albatross is bad luck. That happened right before we left Hono for Guam and the long WESTPAC which was the best damned sea duty of our careers. Although I do sometimes wonder that we've both lived to talk about it."

"Guns, did you ever consider, over the course of the last year and a half, you and I have provided material for sea stories for a whole new generation of Coasties?"

"That ain't no shit, Doc."

"You know Guns, some day when I'm old and tired and can no longer do it, I'm going to write about it, stories about you and me."

"That sounds like a plan. I hope I'm still around to read them."

We went on like that for about three hours. Each of us remembering and relating our favorite stories from the past eighteen months.

"It's getting late and you've got an early day tomorrow, Guns. We best haul ass back to the ship."

"Damn, I guess you're right, shipmate. It's time to go."

The next morning, I met Guns up on the quarter deck. He was looking sharp in his dress blues. I gave him a hug and shook hands with him. Then he threw his sea bag up on his shoulder and I saluted him as he went down the gangway. He climbed into a government van and he was gone. I never saw Guns Gunderson again.

1 THE BEGINNING

My name is Charles D. Williams, chief warrant officer, U.S. Coast Guard, Retired. I'm in my seventies now, an old man, and some of my short-term memories are starting to slip. However, most of the adventures that I experienced during my nearly thirty year Coast Guard career, I can still remember with a fair amount of clarity. I wanted to get some of these stories written down while my memories of them were still intact.

This particular story begins when I was a 26-year-old Independent Duty Hospital Corpsman serving a two-year tour aboard a small Coast Guard cutter in the Pacific. Since it's a sea story, it can only start one way. "This ain't no shit."

The day I was waiting for finally arrived in early September of 1966 when I received orders to a small ship home ported in Honolulu, Hawaii in the Fourteenth Coast Guard District. How this came to pass is a story of its own.

You don't just drop onto a ship that is getting underway for exotic ports of call and high adventure. How I got to this point in my life is a long and convoluted story. I'll give you the short version.

In my attempt to escape from a less than perfect home life, I forged my parent's signature and enlisted in the U.S. Coast Guard Reserves in 1957, right after I turned seventeen. It was a six-by-eight program, six months active duty and 7 ½ years in the reserves. After my initial training, I returned to my home town reserve unit in California and attended monthly weekend meetings, then did two weeks active duty for training each summer. I also moved into my first apartment, got a job, and finished high school at night.

One weekend while I was still on Coast Guard active duty, I was on liberty in New York City. I was wandering around Times Square when I happened upon a crowd surrounding a badly injured man lying on the sidewalk in a pool of his own blood. I was able to use some of my newly-learned first aid skills to save his life. After the ambulance had taken the man away, I was standing in a large circle of people and everybody was patting me on the back and congratulating me. It was a great feeling which turned out to be life-altering for me. Following this incident, I decided to become a hospital corpsman. When I returned to my reserve unit, I took the required correspondence courses and worked in medical clinics during my summer training. I was promoted to hospital corpsman third class in 1960.

5

For the six-year period after my initial six month active duty for training, I did what most of my peer group was doing. I worked at a variety of dead end jobs and partied on weekends.

In November of 1963 when President Kennedy was assassinated, I was working at a casino in Sparks, Nevada near Reno. After the assassination, they closed all the casinos for half a day. With the afternoon off, I found myself out on the sidewalk, with nothing to do. I was leaning against the front wall of my casino just killing time. From the open door of a bar down the street, I could hear the strains of "Blowing in the Wind" playing and there were tears running down my face. After that, I did some serious soul searching.

Like almost everyone else, I thought a lot of President Kennedy. Now, this popular young president was dead. He gave up his life leading our country. And what was I doing? I was almost twenty-four-years-old and I was working at nothing jobs and partying. I decided right then to return to my home town, try finding steady employment, and do something positive with my life, maybe go back to school.

I found a job with an electrical contractor as his parts man. It was a good position, but six months later the union went on a long strike and I was out of a job again. That's when I made the decision to make a career in the Coast Guard. It was the only place where I had anything vested. I had completed six and a half years reserve time. I was a third class petty officer and had finished the correspondence course for second class. There were worse ways of making a living and I figured I could get some more training, a little travel and adventure, and maybe do some good along the way.

My first assignment was to the dispensary at the Coast Guard Training Center in Alameda, California, in the San Francisco Bay Area. It was okay duty and I made some good friends there. One in particular, has lasted a lifetime.

Since I was also steadily employed for at least the next four years, I was able to buy my first new car through the Coast Guard Federal Credit Union. My boss was one of the founders and he helped me arrange the loan to purchase the car. Then, I met a girl and started dating her on a regular basis. Things were going pretty good.

After several months working at the dispensary, I overheard some scuttlebutt that had to do with training and promotions. I began to worry because I had never attended formal hospital corps school. This fact may have a negative impact on my career. After talking to my chief, I decided to put in for the Navy Hospital Corps School in San Diego, California (at the time, there was no HM school in the Coast Guard). When I left for corps school, I didn't want a scene, so I just left. I told

6

my buddies, if the girl I was going out with came around, to tell her that I had been transferred to Alaska on short notice. When you act like an asshole, it always comes back to bite you.

Somebody, one of my buddies, ratted me out and one day my old girlfriend showed up in San Diego looking for me. I guess she caught me in a weak (guilty) moment and I let her talk me into coming back to Alameda after corps school and getting married. I wasn't ready to be married. I had a brand new convertible and had places I wanted to go. In the end though, I wimped out.

I finished school in the summer of 1965, hurried back to Oakland, rented a studio apartment with a Murphy bed, and let the girl's well-to-do father throw us a big wedding. Of the 400 people there, I knew about six of them. We spent a week-long honeymoon in the apartment, screwing.

Then I drove across country to attend a two-month clinical training program at the Coast Guard Academy Hospital in New London, Connecticut. I returned to Alameda in November and was once again assigned to the outpatient clinic. After about two months my new wife and I decided that we really didn't like each other very much and she left. Whew, I dodged the bullet on that one.

I grew up in a dysfunctional family and I sure wasn't ready to start one of my own. My ex-wife moved to the Haight Ashbury District in San Francisco and became a hippie. A few months later, I took and passed the hospital corpsman second class exam and was promoted on 1 July 1966.

My first order of business after being promoted was to finish my correspondence course and take the first class exam. Then I put in for an independent duty assignment aboard any ship that was home ported in Honolulu, Hawaii. To my everlasting surprise, later that year, I got the orders I asked for. It was an HM1 billet. I figured I got the job because I had already taken and passed the first class petty officer test and would probably be promoted shortly after reporting aboard my new unit.

The adventure begins:

When I climbed aboard the TWA DC8 in San Francisco, I was resplendent in my first set of "Tailor Made Gabardine Blues." Eighteen-inch bells with dragons on my cuffs and a big mermaid embroidered inside my thirteen button fly. My low cuts were spit shined, my neckerchief was cinched up tight, and the wings in my Dixie Cup hat were just right.

I was a, by God, second class petty officer, a non-commissioned officer with two chevrons under my crow and two hash marks on my left

7

sleeve. The two lonely ribbons on my chest represented the National Defense and Expert Rifleman medals. I was on my way to my first independent duty corpsman assignment.

As an independent duty corpsman, you were considered to be an advanced corpsman capable of providing primary, and if necessary, prolonged medical care to personnel on ships at sea and on isolated shore stations overseas. I guess we'd see about that. All I knew was that I would be pretty much on my own. My training and experience, I had some, including a year of working graveyard shift in a civilian hospital emergency room. Was it enough? It was too late to worry about that now. It was sink or swim and I was ready for the challenge.

The plane ride over turned out to be a real hoot. It was what they called red, white, and blue service. This is how they designated first, second, and third class seats. Since I was an enlisted man traveling on a government TR, travel request, I was assigned a seat in last class. As it turned out this October flight was right in the middle of the off season. Since there were only twenty or thirty people on board, as soon as the wheels were up, the stewardesses abolished the class system and broke out the champagne. We had a party all the way to Honolulu.

Several hours and a couple magnums of champagne later, I stood, a bit unsteadily, in the door of the plane at Honolulu International Airport.

It was warm and humid and smelled of tropical flowers and pineapple. I could hear the sound of Hawaiian music playing. There were pretty hula girls with flower leis at the bottom of the boarding ladder. We all got a kiss on the cheek and a happy "Aloha" while beautiful flower leis were placed over our heads. I was thinking, *why did I waste all those years living on the mainland?*

I grabbed a cab and we zipped down the Kamehameha Highway to Keehi Lagoon Road and then Sand Island Road and into the Sand Island Coast Guard Base. It was just what I had expected, a place for sailors. There were six 180-foot buoy tenders; two destroyer-sized white cutters, and a boat house with three or four 40-foot patrol boats. And one of the Coast Guards' old one of a kind fleet, the black hulled freighter Kukui. She was the ship that built the Fourteenth District, literally. Across the channel at Pier Four, I could see a Coast Guard 95-foot patrol boat.

I shouldered my sea bag up the brow of the *Basswood*, saluted, and announced to the quarterdeck watch that I was reporting for duty. The OOD snapped my salute back and said "Welcome aboard, Doc." A little shiver went up my spine as I thought, *'Shit, that's me he's talking to. I'm the Doc.'*

8

I did not know quite what to expect. I had done a reserve cruise on the 311-foot *Unimak* in 1957 and some reserve active duty on the 327-foot *Taney* in 1960 but that was as a deck ape (seaman), not as a petty officer. The only buoy tender I had ever seen was on a training tour of an old steam tender back on the east coast almost nine years earlier.

The first thing I noticed about the *Basswood* was that she was decked out like a yacht. The ship was well-maintained and super clean. On the outside, much of the machinery and trim was industrial chrome, polished brass, and fancywork. There was an awning over the entire fantail, from the quarter deck all the way aft to the stern rail. There were two beautiful wood benches whose seats and backs were upholstered in international orange leatherette.

As I followed the messenger watch below, I found that it was just as nice inside with the addition of stainless steel backing on all the ladders. On the mess deck everything was white, including the deck. The curtains and mess table seats were matching international orange. I was thinking, *this is a working ship?*

Yeah, it was. The work the crew performed was hard and dirty, the hours were long, and it was often dangerous. The *Basswood*'s missions required her to spend months of underway time traveling to almost every corner of the Pacific. And yet this ship that was built in 1943 was neat as a pin, it looked new, there was no running rust anywhere, and she far outshined her sister ships at the dock. The only explanation for this was the commanding officer and the caliber of professional seamen in key positions aboard the *Basswood*, starting with the chief boatswain's mate.

The first captain I served with was Jonathon Liam Quinn III. He was a Merchant Marine Academy graduate with the rank of commander. That was a lot of horsepower (rank) for such a small ship. He was a little over six feet tall with a full head of thick, wavy, steel gray hair. Captain Quinn was a very striking gentleman.

He actually looked more like he belonged on the bridge of a luxury liner, rather than a buoy tender. The captain lived aboard and often entertained lady friends in his cabin. It was his yacht.

He was aloof in his dealings with the crew, not a sailor's skipper, but he ran a tight ship and there was never any question of his abilities as a seaman. One thing we all came to appreciate about Captain Quinn was his rank. Whenever we were working around Pearl Harbor and sleek Navy Destroyers passed us, they would have to render side honors. The skipper on our little black tub of a ship outranked theirs. You could see it

9

on their faces as they manned the rails of their ships, the Navy guys hated this. We loved it.

When I reported aboard, they were in the process of rotating some major crew members. Crew changes are a continual ongoing process on Coast Guard ships. I actually served with two sets of officers and senior enlisted personnel during my time on the *Basswood*, as well as an almost entirely new deck force and engineering crew. So, everybody aboard, including yours truly, was busy getting acquainted with the ship, their shipmates, and their new duties.

When I first saw the sick bay it looked to me as if it had not been well cared for by my predecessors. It was not up to the standard of the rest of the ship. This is how I spent my first couple of weeks, setting the sick bay ship-shape. I replaced the old chipped floor tile, repaired the lagging on the overhead and bulkheads, and painted the whole place. After that, I started looking around to see what there was to do on the island of Oahu.

2 LIBERTY IN HONOLULU

Before I hooked up with Guns Gunderson, my liberties in Honolulu weren't too spectacular. My car had not arrived and I didn't know anyone so my running mates were a bunch of young guys from the deck force. Their idea of a good time was pretty straight forward. Drink as much beer as you could, raise hell down on Waikiki Beach, and try and pick up *haole* girls from the mainland. Like that was going to happen.

It was the mid-sixties, we had short hair, and we were servicemen. Mostly, we ended up on Sandy Beach down by the Blow Hole, body surfing, barbequing chicken, and drinking even more beer. At the end of a long day and night of this kind of liberty, you would go back to the ship, shitfaced, sticky with salt from the ocean and sunburned. Then, you'd jump in the rain locker, take a shower, and hit the rack. Some of the guys found relief making love to their socks.

Guns had arrived five or six months before me and already had a couple of liberty buddies he hung with.

They had chipped in on a beater car and month-to-month rental of a room at the old rundown roach-infested Islander Hotel, or the Roach Hotel, as everyone called it. It was located behind The International Market Place, near an area known as the Jungle. At any rate, it was someplace to go drink Primo, the cheap local beer. We could buy Primo at the base exchange for less than $3.00 a case and got about $0.75 back on a case of empties when you returned them to the brewery. I remember one time we had 57 cases of empties on the landing by the front door of our room. We used the refund to finance a party. At any rate, the old Gunner seemed to have the liberty situation in Honolulu all scoped out.

Guns and I were both on the promotion list for petty officer first class. One day shortly after I reported aboard, he came up to me and introduced himself.

"Hey Doc, my name's Gunderson. I'm the gunner's mate. I heard you and I are probably going to be making first class together. I thought I'd better introduce myself, and maybe give you some tips on liberty here in Hono."

"Hi Guns, glad to meet you and I would welcome any advice you could give me about the liberty situation."

Guns Gunderson, and the arrival of my 1965 Corvair convertible, changed my world. For starters, the car was red, but I found out island girls were partial to orange. So, I had the car painted international orange. Then, Guns pointed out to me that it was a waste of time trying to pick up *haole* chicks on Waikiki Beach, something I had already found out the hard way.

He said, "Go native, son. Hit the local Korean and Japanese bars, learn a little of the language, eat the food, and get into the culture."

The master spoke and I learned.

Guns taste in women was eclectic, but while we were in Honolulu he was going with a gal named Josie. She worked nights at an old WWII watering hole called the Two Jacks Bar on South Hotel Street, or, if you prefer, Shit Street. Josie was a nice gal with a pretty face and shiny black hair. She was Royal Hawaiian in stature (large) and her body resembled nothing so much as our ships towing bit wearing a muumuu.

Guns originally came from the midwest. He was skinny, about 5' 10", had white blonde hair, and glacier blue eyes. They made quite a contrast, but they were happy, so who cares? Josie also fixed me up with some of her not-so large girl friends from time to time.

An average evening on liberty in Honolulu, after I started hanging with Guns, might include hitting happy hour at the Sand Island EM Club. Then, drinking with the girls at Two Jacks until the bar closed at 0200. After that, we would all go to Tin Tin's in China Town, actually just across the street, and eat Chinese food until we were stuffed.

It was a good thing that we were pretty shit-faced, so the sight of the ancient Chinese woman making wonton on the table next to us did not turn us off. She was always there, sitting beside a two-foot high mound of ground pork being blown by countless flies. She smoked a cigarette with an inch-long ash, which she never removed from her mouth.

She would snatch up a glob of pork with a wonton wrapper, squeeze it shut with her fingers, and throw it in a large basin on the floor next to her feet. Yum, actually their food was very good, sanitary no, but it tasted good. When we were done eating, if we did not feel like turning in for the night, we would sometimes go skinny dipping at Alamoana Park.

When my car arrived, I started frequenting a couple of Japanese bars and a Korean bar called the New Paris Café. I was the only round eye (Caucasian) who patronized these places. The Asian bar girls were fascinated with my sun-bleached blonde hair, as well as the hair on my arms. They would keep bringing me Pu Pu's (bar snacks), just to watch a Caucasian eat with chop sticks. This, and the fact that I would eat anything, went a long way to increase my currency with the Korean and Japanese bar girls. Being that I was the only round eye that patronized these places also helped.

Over the next few months, I dated several girls out of the New Paris Café. One of those was Cho Sin, a five-foot-ten-inch beauty from Pusan, Korea. She had married a G.I. to get into the States, and then ditched him. She had beautiful long black hair that went all the way down past her butt. Neither of us had any misconceptions about the nature of our relationship. We just concentrated on having a good time.

In my further attempt to go multi-cultural, I joined a couple of my buddies and started taking Jujitsu and Judo lessons. We found a traditional *dojo* over on the North side of the island.

The *sensei* was impressed with us. He thought that we were quick studies and he spent a lot of time with us. He even brought Judo mats over to our ship so we could practice when we were away. By the time our homeport was changed to Guam, I was well on my way to my Brown Belt.

Island life agreed with me. I spent my liberty nights drinking with Guns and some of the other guys at the Two Jacks, or at the Roach Hotel. On weekends, I explored the island of Oahu in my bright orange convertible, often with Cho Sin at my side, or I would take her to Fort Derussey, an Army recreation center located on some of the best real estate on Waikiki Beach.

Cho Sin had a bikini that was the same color as my car. She sure looked good in it and even better out of it. One of her favorite things to do at the beach was to run out into the surf. When she was waist deep she would remove her bikini bottom and wave it at me, as if to say 'hurry up slow poke.' I often wondered if the kids snorkeling in the area might have seen something besides fish and sea shells.

Guns and I just sort of meshed as shipmates. He was about seven years older than I and he had done it all. He was kind of a service hermit, not married, stayed on ships as much as he could, and liked the overseas ports. I'd known or heard of a number of guys like him. One old corpsman, for instance "Pappy Morehouse", made chief and sought no higher promotion. He rode the white cutters until he was 65 and they made him retire.

We had another one aboard the *Basswood* for a short while, a first class quartermaster named Cecil Robards.

He never even went ashore except to put his pay in one of the five banks he had accounts with in Honolulu. He hated being in port because you had to pay to get your laundry done. The ship's laundry was not in operation while the ship was in port.

They say he was rich, and as tight as he was, I could believe it. I think he only had one pair of skivvies, which he used for pajamas. When he shaved, he used razor blades that the other crewmembers had thrown away. He would sharpen them in a shot glass. Robards used rainbow soap to shower with. He collected all the little pieces of soap the other guys left in the soap trays in the showers and compressed them together, thus, rainbow soap.

His favorite meal was a horse cock sandwich, G.I. bologna with mustard between two slices of bread. He did not stay aboard any of the ships long. As his current ship was returning to port from one WESTPAC, he would be on the signal lights talking to the Quartermasters on the next ship leaving to see if he could get a lateral transfer and head right back out to sea again. It kind of looked like I was heading down that same road, using the Guns model, not Robards'.

Guns Gunderson had served as a gunner's mate in the Navy during the Korean War and had spent a lot of years in the Pacific. He was one of the old-time sailors. He could do anything, but he was not a test taker, and the new service-wide promotion exam took a toll on guys like Guns. That's why we were making first class at the same time. I don't think any of that bothered him as long as he could find a seagoing billet.

I guess the other thing we had in common is that we were both single and on independent duty. Each of us was the only one in our particular specialties aboard the ship. Gunderson was the only gunner's mate and I was the only hospital corpsman. He had his weapons and the armory to care for and the crew to train in gunnery. I had my sick bay and the health and well-being of the crew to look after, as well as training them in personal hygiene, first aid, and casualty control. We were both going to be very busy at these tasks in the near future, something neither of us knew yet. As time went by, we would find even more reasons to respect each other.

3 WHAT BUOY TENDERS DO

Well, I can assure you it wasn't all fun and games. The seagoing buoy tenders have traditionally been the work horses of the Coast Guard fleet. The 180-foot tenders come in three classes; A, B, or C, depending on when they were built. The designations represented evolutionary changes to the ships over time. The *Basswood* was a C Class. All of these types of ship were named after either a kind of shrub or a tree; *Basswood, Ironwood, Buttonwood, Planetree, Mallow,* etc.

About the ships: The 180-foot buoy tenders were black-hulled seagoing vessels that were designed and created to establish and maintain aids to navigation. These aids included sea buoys, channel buoys, harbor buoys, channel markers, day boards, and other aids required to safely guide boats and ships operating in navigable waters. These tenders did their work in many places around the world, wherever the United States had an interest. They were built to operate in all kinds of weather, and, for that reason, had ice breaker hulls.

The Class C buoy tenders had two large holds to carry supplies and equipment, and a large boom to handle buoys and cargo.

The *Basswood* had diesel electric engines and a single screw and was capable of towing much larger ships. She was not fast or highly maneuverable, but she got us there. She had a sustained top speed of 11.9 knots and could get up to 15 knots in an emergency. We usually cruised between 9 and 11 knots.

Our operating area in the Fourteenth Coast Guard District included the South Pacific and the West Pacific all the way to Asia and the Orient. In addition to maintaining buoys and channel markers, we also serviced light houses and provided logistic support for LORAN Stations (Long Range Aids to Navigation). These stations put out a radio signal that allowed ships and airplanes equipped with LORAN receivers to plot their position.

We were available for search and rescue missions in our operating area, as well as occasional typhoon relief. If required, I was available to provide emergency medical aid, as able, to civilian populations living in remote coastal villages or on small islands. Since we were a small ship and able to navigate where other ships could not go, we were occasionally tasked to provide transportation for researchers and wildlife scientists. This provided some very interesting work for the ship and crew and took us to places where few had ever been.

One of the first things we were called on to do, subsequent to my reporting aboard, was to assist a freighter in distress. It actually turned out to be pretty funny. We were tied up at our usual berth at the Sand Island Coast Guard Base. Guns and I were sitting back on the fantail, shooting the shit, and enjoying a cup of coffee. That's what riders did. What are riders, you ask?

Riders are what the rest of the crew called those of us who did not have actual hands-on roles in the operation of the ship. The operators would be the bridge gang, deck force, and engine room guys. The riders would include the corpsman, gunner's mate, supply clerk, and the ship's yeoman.

After I held sick call and did my daily sanitation inspections, I was pretty much done for the day unless there was a medical emergency. Guns had even less to do, so they made him the master-at-arms and put him in charge of the compartment cleaners and mess cooks. They could not have found a better guy for the MAA job. Gunderson was an easygoing guy who guided his charges by explaining why something had to be done, and then showing them how to do it. He never once had to scream at or berate them to get the job done. Other than that, he had to keep his guns in good repair and oiled. He also gave gunnery instruction, but that was mostly when we were underway.

"So, Guns what do you have in mind when they grant liberty today?"

"I thought I'd stop at the EM Club and catch Happy Hour and then go to the apartment over at the Roach Hotel, maybe get something to eat and then go down to Shit Street. You want to tag along?"

"Sure. I've got nothing better to do. Cho Sin is working tonight."

"Yeah, we best get it while we can. Next week we go to underway training and that will mess up liberty for a couple of weeks."

"Oh yeah, shit, I forgot about that. I'm glad I cleaned up sick bay when I reported aboard, and my medical equipment and supplies are pretty much up to date.

I've got a couple more crew training sessions on casualty control to get done before we get over to Pearl."

Just then, all hell broke loose. The claxon was sounding General Quarters and special sea detail was being piped over the 1MC (public address system). *Now what the hell's going on*, I wondered?

As one of the crewmembers ran by on the way to his special sea detail assignment, he said, "There's a liberty ship with a hole in its main hold and we were going to provide assistance."

I got up to go to my detail, fantail talker, about ten feet away from where we were sitting. The fantail talker was hooked up to the bridge by sound-powered phone. His job was to keep the captain advised on the status of the aft line handlers and to report that everyone was in their place and doing their jobs in preparation for getting underway.

As I went to my detail I said to Guns, "I guess we can cancel our liberty plans for a while."

"Yep, well, saving folks is what we do, Doc."

Liberty ships were specifically built during and for the Second World War. They probably helped win the war. They were 441-foot cheaply built cargo ships and we were producing them at a rate of one a day during the war. They hauled cargo and troops as well as war machines. Many were lost during the war, many were scrapped afterwards, but there were still a lot of them out there hauling freight for small shipping companies or third world countries. Many were rust buckets that did not belong at sea.

This one was several hundred miles off shore and still underway bound for Honolulu.

One of our planes had air-dropped them some extra dewatering pumps and we were underway at our best speed to intercept her, assist as necessary, and then escort her into port. When we arrived, she was listing a little to her starboard side. A forklift had come loose from its tie downs in heavy weather and drove the tines through the ship's hull below the waterline, and she was taking on water.

We sent a damage control detail aboard with some additional pumps to assess the damage and do what they could. The forklift was heavy and was stuck solid and could not be easily moved. With the extra pumps working and fair weather predicted, it was decided that we would leave the forklift in place and just escort her into Honolulu.

The humorous thing about this mission was a statement the captain of the stricken merchant vessel made. Okay, the fact that we refer to all of our ships as cutters gives the impression of speed. Cutter equals fast ship. As I mentioned before, our buoy tender could make only 15 knots in a following sea with a tailwind and we were cranking out those 15 knots and sweating bullets to get them.

At one point, the merchant ship's captain made the following radio call: "Coast Guard, if we're holding you up, I can get my ship up to 17 knots." And that was the laugh around the bar when we finally got on liberty later that night. The stricken vessel we were saving beat us into port.

4 SICK CALL

My daily routine in sick bay was just that, pretty routine. I'd get sniffles and sneezes, minor injuries from work on the buoy deck or in the engine room, or maybe something they had done on liberty. Of course, there was always the humorous stuff. One day, a seaman named Grant reported to sick bay with an extremely swollen left forearm and hand with red streaks running up his arm.

"What the hell did you do to yourself Grant?"

"I got bit by a scorpion last week Doc, so I took out my knife and cut an X over the bite and sucked the poison out, like you see them do in the movies," he said, all proud of himself.

"You stupid fuck. You've got cellulites. You could lose your arm doing something like that."

I was thinking *some of the kids you find in the lower ranks must wear a size two white hat. This guy Grant obviously had the IQ of a house plant.*

Number one, the scorpions here on the islands have a sting about the same as a honey bee. The knife he used to do the "John Wayne" on his arm was filthy, way more poisonous than the sting. So, I gave the guy a lecture while I cleaned and dressed his wound. Then I gave him a shot in the ass with several million units of penicillin.

Sick Call would be held at 0800 in the morning and after officer's call to quarters at 1330 in the afternoon. The rest of my time was spent cleaning and sterilizing instruments, making sanitation and food handler inspections, and writing reports. That was not a lot to do, and it gave me time to watch buoy operations and to check out the rest of the departments aboard ship, and see what the other guys did for a living.

The more you knew about what the other crewmembers did aboard a small ship like ours, the better. You could never tell when some kind of an emergency might happen and one or more of your shipmates could be injured or lost. When this happened, someone would have to fill in for them. For that reason, there was a lot of cross-training held onboard small Coast Guard ships.

One other kid that cracked me up every time I saw him in sick bay was Seaman Apprentice Godfrey. He was new aboard, a tall, skinny kid who could not figure out how to get through hatches without hitting his head on the knife edge. I stitched up wounds on his forehead and hairline three times in his first couple of weeks onboard. He had so many stitches that he was starting to look handmade, like some kind of Frankenstein.

18

You do a lot of drilling on ships, which means moving rapidly fore and aft through many watertight doors or hatches. The watertight doors are left latched open, except in emergencies. The doors themselves have a rubber gasket all around the outside edge.

The door openings have a corresponding lip or knife edge that creates a watertight seal when the door is closed. These doorways are not very big, and there is a high door sill that you have to step over. If you're short to average, it's usually not a problem. If you're tall, you have to remember to duck at the same time you step over the door sill. Godfrey was not too coordinated and had a hell of a time stepping and ducking at the same time.

Since I was the Doc, and at twenty-seven older than most of the crew, there was another duty which fell to me. I became a counselor, of sorts. They came to me with all kinds of personal problems, problems on the ship, problems at home, and girl problems. You name it. I attempted to give them the best advice I could. Hey, they were my guys and it was my job to take care of them, a responsibility that I took very seriously.

One day in port as I sat in sick bay reviewing some health records, one of the deck crew came running down the passageway, yelling "Doc, Doc, Jones is up on the flying bridge and he's threatening to jump."

Oh shit, I thought, *Jones is another one of the new guys. Well, I handled a few suicide attempts when I was assigned to the boot camp in Alameda. Let's see what this guy's problem is.* I've found that suicide attempts among young coast guardsmen are usually caused by one of two things; either the guy is not adapting well to the rigors and discipline of military life, or he got a Dear John letter from his girlfriend back home.

I went up to the bridge of the ship and looked over at Seaman Apprentice Jones. He was hanging from the flying bridge rail. I asked him, "What's the problem, Jones?"

"Don't come up here or I'll jump."

"Come on, you don't want to do that."

"Yes I do and I will, I will."

After a few minutes of this I finally said, "Look Jones, it's hot out here and I've got other stuff to do. If you're going to jump, jump and get it over with. One of two things will happen, if you clear the ship, you'll get wet, if you don't, you're going to break some bones and be in terrible pain."

"You're fucking crazy," Jones responded.

"No, I just think that you really don't want to do this. Why don't you climb down from there and come to sick bay and we'll have a chat.

19

When we get done, if you still want to commit suicide, I'll show you how to do it right. Come on, get down from there."

Luckily, he did climb down and come to sick bay with me. We had a long talk. Just as I had thought, his high school sweetheart had found another guy and he had just received a Dear John letter from her informing him of this.

I guaranteed him that the first one of those little Asian girls he hooked up with on our forthcoming WESTPAC would make him forget all about his girl back home. When he left sick bay, he was no longer thinking about "Suzie State Side", but rather about getting laid for the first time in the exotic ports we were going to be visiting.

When we did hit these ports, it caused yet another problem with Jones and several of our other new young Coasties. They all wanted to marry the first one or two of the Asian girls they slept with. I guess you really couldn't blame them. Some of these young sailors had never even had a serious kiss from a girl.

All of a sudden, here they were, surrounded by thousands of dainty young Asian girls their own age. Each one prettier than the next, girls who knew how to make a guy feel like King Kong, and who could fulfill every sexual fantasy in their teenage heads.

The last thing Jones said to me when he left sick bay, "You are crazy, Doc."

I responded, "Yeah, maybe, but you're not out there lying on the deck bleeding and screaming and wishing you hadn't done it."

The space where I performed my medical miracles was located on the port side of the ship between the crews head and the Chief's berthing area. It consisted of two compartments. The smaller of the two had a shitter, or commode, if you prefer. In the large compartment, as you entered to the right, was a full-sized autoclave for sterilizing instruments and surgical packs. There was a wash basin, a desk with file drawers, and a typewriter well containing an old Royal typewriter. These were all located right up against the hull, or port side of the compartment.

On the inboard side of the compartment, there were two bunks that were much more substantial than those you would find in the crews berthing, and that had actual mattresses with fans mounted on the bulkhead at the foot of each bunk. I slept in the top one. There was a large cabinet on the aft bulkhead where I kept my medical supplies, as well as a microscope and other lab equipment.

There were two portholes in the main compartment and one in the head. I took a couple of GI shit cans and had the damage controlman fashion them into air scoops that fit into the portholes to get some fresh air into sick bay. The only problem with that was from time to time we

20

would catch a rogue wave and this would provide me with some fresh salt water as well.

It would get in my old typewriter and I had a hell of a time keeping it rust free. I finally started spraying it with the spray we used on the machine guns, some military forerunner of WD-40.

There was no treatment table in the sick bay, so, for the minor stuff I had the patients sit on a chair while I worked on them. If it was more serious, and they had to lie down, I put them in the lower berth. That was about it. It was sufficient for my needs while I was aboard. If something really bad happens, you always hope you are somewhere where you can get a medivac helicopter or plane in. Most of the time, we weren't. As a Coast Guard independent duty corpsman, you basically just sucked it up and did it.

5 BUOY OUT ON MOLOKAI

One of the next call outs the *Basswood* received was a buoy out on the island of Molokai. The sea buoy leading into Molokai Harbor had no light and we were dispatched to repair it. There was not much on Molokai. For many years it was a feared leper colony. Starting back in the early days of colonization, when lepers were found in the community, they would be rounded up and taken by ship over to Molokai and tossed over the side. There they would have to swim ashore and fend for themselves. Leprosy was a very fearful thing in the early days in Hawaii. That's understandable when people started losing body part like ears, noses, fingers, and so on.

Today, there are still Lepers there as well as a leprosy treatment facility, but people now understand that leprosy is not highly contagious as once was thought. There is also a small town and of interest to us, a couple of bars. These were bars where it might not be in good taste to order two fingers of anything.

It was a two-day trip over and back. We would cross the Molokai Channel, haul the buoy out of the water, repair and service it, and put it back on station. Then, tie up overnight and return to Hono the next day. That evening, after we tied up and liberty was granted, I went ashore and had a few drinks at one of the two local bars. Guns had JOOD duty on the quarter deck.

That night, when I returned to the ship, Guns said, "Boy, do I have a story for you."

"Yeah, what happened?" I asked.

"The XO and the Bosun got into it."

"No shit?"

I suppose this would be a good place to tell you about the first XO and warrant bosun that I served with. They were both of Italian descent. The Executive Officer LCDR Guido Strozza and the First Lieutenant Warrant Bosun Emil Cantatore had both come up through the ranks. The XO had once been a warrant bosun like Mr. Cantatore and I think they had a history. They worked fine together when there was work to be done, but during liberty hours if we were someplace where there was only one bar, one of them stayed on the ship. If there were two or more bars, then they drank in separate drinking establishments. They must have crossed paths this night.

Guns said, "The XO came up the gangway under a full head of steam and told me to go to the recreation locker, break out two sets of boxing gloves, and bring them to the wardroom. Mr. Cantatore was right behind him." Guns said, "After I delivered the gloves, I ran back down to the dock and peeked through the wardroom porthole."

"They knocked each other back and forth across the wardroom until their arms got tired and then they turned in for the night. I couldn't tell which one of them won. They both got some good licks in"

I always thought it was pretty gutsy of the XO, taking on the bosun. The XO was an average size guy. CWO Cantatore looked like a combination of Smokey the Bear and a bad-ass Marine. He was big all over with a marine haircut. He had no neck, just these massive arms that seemed to protrude from the base of his head. He looked like a big bear stuffed into a set of khakis. I would not have fought him if I could have used someone else's body.

The rest of the trip was uneventful. We tied up the next afternoon back at Sand Island, hit the beach, and made it to happy hour at the EM Club. A place to drink was never a problem in Honolulu. If you did not feel like going to the civilian bars, the island had a bunch of military drinking establishments, including five of the best NCO Clubs in the world. There was so much military on the island of Oahu, I sometimes wondered how they made room for the tourists and the locals.

It was still a great place to be home ported at the time. There was a lot to do, but if you wanted to get away from the crowds, there were still places where you could do it. Makaha was one such place and the North Shore was another. The only people you would find at these locations were a few locals and some serious surfers. We're talking Wiamea Bay and the Banzi Pipe Line.

6 UNDERWAY TRAINING

The next two days after the Molokai run, I drilled the crew and liter bearers. I drilled them in casualty control and other things they would need to know in the case of a combat situation or a major emergency. We would be tested on this during our two weeks of underway training, which started the following Monday.

I had a unique way of getting the crew's attention during my classes. If I caught someone who was skylarking (not paying attention), I would declare that person a casualty. Then, I would place him up on the flying bridge and assign a couple of the biggest fuck ups on the ship to go and rescue him, closely supervised, of course. Hey, it worked.

Well, Monday came and we got underway early and made the short trip over to Pearl Harbor and tied up in the small ship area where the Navy tied up their seagoing tugs, mine sweepers, and submarine rescue ships. Then, we were boarded by both Navy and Coast Guard personnel from fleet training, who would put us through our paces.

We would be drilled in all our shipboard evolutions. These would include, General Quarters, simulated combat, damage control, man overboard, navigation, casualty control and medical procedures, and much, much more. Most of this was done underway. We would start early in the morning and return and tie up late in the day. For a couple of the evolutions we had to stay out over night.

Coast Guard ships go through this training every year. For small ships, it lasted two weeks. For larger cutters, it was a month. It was pretty intense stuff and it created a lot of stress and anxiety. Sometimes tempers got short. Of course, in keeping with our motto of Semper Paratus (always ready), we had a remedy for that. Our remedy also maintained our reputation with the Navy guys that we really were hooligans and modern day pirates and not to be trifled with.

I don't know who thought of this, but it worked. On a buoy tender, you have a large forward deck where you bring the, sometime very large, buoys aboard to service and paint them. To facilitate this, there is a buoy port. A section of upper hull about ten or twelve feet wide could be lifted out on either side of the ship. When this section was out, there was nothing between the buoy deck and the water below.

The deck force would remove one of these sections and then tie a piece of twenty-one thread (one inch) nylon line to each side of the buoy port, leaving enough slack so crewmembers could hold it up and form sort of a boxing ring. Guys who had a pissing match going or a grudge could take each other on in the ring. Others did it just for the hell of it or to release tension.

This was not boxing or wrestling. It was a grappling match. The closest thing I can compare it to was Japanese Sumo. Two combatants would get into the ring and one would try to force the other over the side and into the water. Often, they both went in. If it was taking too long, the crew surrounding the ring would surge forward and push them over the side. We did this every afternoon after we got in from training and tied up. The Navy sailors would line the rails of their ships and holler and cheer while they watched us. I think they were, for the most part, aghast that anything so rowdy and fun could ever happen on a military vessel. We loved it.

I lucked out during my phase of the training. The medical instructor was a Navy senior chief hospital corpsman. He was a sub sailor and had never served on a surface ship. Submarines don't buck and roll like surface ships and buoy tenders are the worst. They are shaped like a bathtub. With the ice breaker configured hull, they buck, roll, and wallow. If you are even slightly susceptible to sea sickness, you don't want to be anywhere near a buoy tender at sea. Well, the senior chief was one seasick puppy. I gave him the latest seasick medications of the day before we got underway, which didn't help much, and then I spent most of the day caring for him.

I got an "outstanding" in the medical phase of our training. He told the XO that I was the best HM2 he had ever seen. This put me in a very good place with the XO and CO as these training results reflect directly on how well they were doing their jobs. The ship got an overall grade of "excellent" and the skipper got to paint a couple of big Es on our stack, a white one for deck and a red one for engineering. Back to Sand Island we went, with everybody feeling good about our performance, and ready for some liberty.

There is a funny phenomenon among sailors. When you're on the ship, all you talk about is pussy. When you are ashore sitting in a bar, all you talk about is the ship. Well, she was an ugly duckling as ships go, but she was our ship and we loved her and would spill blood defending her.

At the end of the year, the *Basswood* was rated as the best ship in the Pacific for 1966. We had received the highest Refresher Training score of any ship, Coast Guard or Navy, that had gone through training at Pearl Harbor that year. Go figure. A bunch of hooligans like us pulling that off.

25

7 THE BIRD WATCHER PATROL

The Bird Watcher Patrol happens about once a year, occasionally more often. One or the other of the Honolulu buoy tenders was always tasked with providing transportation on these trips because the vessels were the most suited to the work. The trips lasted about forty-five days and for the crew it was a fishing trip and some of the best beachcombing anywhere. This was followed up by a two-day drunk on Midway Island, and then back home.

Everybody knows about the tourist Hawaii, but most people don't know that the Hawaiian Islands continue in a chain of uninhabited atolls and islands all the way out to Midway Island. They are national fish and wildlife preserves populated by many species of rare birds, as well as the endangered Hawaiian monk seal. The islands and the waters for three miles around them are off limits for fishing or trespassing.

The islands are basically untouched by human hands, except for these trips by biologists for the purpose of counting birds and placing leg bands on some of them.

They also moved nesting pairs of certain birds to try and get them established on other islands. On this trip there were also a couple of marine biologists who were counting and tagging the seals.

On the way out, we stopped at Kauai in the picturesque port of Nawiliwili. Back in the day of Captain Ahab and *Moby Dick*, Nawiliwili was a popular port for the old wooden whaling ships. Kauai is the northernmost of the populated Hawaiian Islands and was the last to accept rule under King Kamehameha. We also passed Niihau, the seventh largest of the Hawaiian Islands. It's privately owned and populated only by pure Hawaiians to preserve the cultural heritage of Hawaii.

Then, we proceeded to the islands to be worked. These included Nihoa, Necker, French Frigate Shoals, Gardner, Laysan, Lisianski, Pearl, and Hermes Reef and Midway. The unpopulated islands range from the peaks of undersea mountains to coral formed islands and atolls that are only a few feet above sea level. Some have a moderate amount of foliage. Others have very little vegetation.

They all have many kinds of birds. Some, like the Laysan teal, are found only on these islands. When the actual wildlife work started, the scientists would go ashore and do their thing. While they were doing that, we would fish off of the fantail and catch Pacific tuna. They were called *ulua* and got to be about seventy pounds.

When I landed a nice one, Guns came up to me and said, "Get the stew burners (cooks) to put that in the freezer. At some of the small islands in the Trust Territories and the Palau Islands, you can get a girl and take care of your whole liberty with one of those fish."

"They love them. At least that's what I've been told. You know Doc, some of the places we'll be visiting are going to be virgin territory even for me."

I figured that what he had heard was probably right, and had the cooks stow my fish. Pretty soon the sharks were attracted to our fishing activities. Some of the guys started to haul them aboard and cut out their eyes and jaws to sell to tourist shops back in Hawaii. I didn't much care for the idea.

When the scientists finished their work, after first being admonished not to bother the birds or seals, we were allowed to go ashore a handful at a time so we would not put too much pressure on the animals. Some of the guys had no interest in going ashore, so only a few of us went. It was amazing. The animals had so little contact with humans that they did not know that they should be afraid of us. If you walked slowly, you could walk among them without them taking flight. I found a good spot and sat down and watched these birds and seals go about their daily lives as if I were not there. It was a great experience. I was also able to take photos of a monk seal and her pup, fairy terns, brown breasted boobies, albatross, and great frigate birds.

The beaches were pristine and the beachcombing was fantastic. I found a few nice Japanese glass fishing floats with nice netting on them, and also a few interesting sea shells and pieces of driftwood. The fishing floats come from Japanese open ocean drift nets. They range in size from a softball to larger than a basketball. They can be found in different shades of glass like amber, blue, green, and plain. One with a nice net could bring you about $35.00 dollars if you sold it to a Waikiki tourist shop.

They would turn around and peddle them to the tourists for $150.00 or more.

And yes, I did kill an albatross while I was trolling as we steamed from one island to another. Much to the chagrin of the scientists and bird watchers who were looking on. Once it was tangled in my wire leader, there was nothing I could do but pull the dead bird aboard.

The trip ended at Midway, the site of a major naval battle during WWII and the home of a fair-sized naval base. Midway was also a major nesting ground for albatross. They would be setting on their mud nests everywhere. You had to walk around and through them to get anywhere.

27

The bird watchers kept track of the birds they had counted by spraying their heads with a fluorescent red dye. I have to tell you, coming back from the EM Club at night half-shitfaced was a surreal experience. All you would see were these reddish orange dots about eighteen inches off the ground, waving back and forth in the dark.

The stop at French Frigate Shoals was kind of fun and worth mention here. French Frigate was a Coast Guard LORAN station. The station itself consisted of nothing but an airstrip with three small station buildings at one end with a reef all around. From the air, the place resembles an aircraft carrier. Fifteen men spend one solid year out there with next to nothing to do. The waters around the station were teeming with fish and they were also teeming with sharks. There was also a small rookery of monk seals there, and the biologists wanted to count them.

These biologists may have been good at what they did, but they were lacking in common sense, like most academics. They had a brand new runabout, probably purchased with grant money. The skipper offered them a coxswain to operate the boat for them. He told them that there were some tricky tides and currents to watch out for. They listened to him impatiently and then turned him down and insisted on operating their own boat.

With that, they motored off to the station small boat channel. They tied their boat up at one of the pilings that held up the pier and went off to do their work. While they were gone, the current drifted the boat under the pier and the tide came in and crushed the entire superstructure of their boat and ruined the outboard engine. It must have been a humiliating and humbling experience for them to then have to come to skipper and beg him for the use of one of our ship's small boats and a coxwain.

One half of this dynamic duo was a knockout Scandinavian-looking babe with white blonde hair and a great body. You could not miss her body because she was wearing an itty bitty white bikini and strolling around the station. I guess she did not notice, or maybe she did notice the group of station personnel following her around with their tongues hanging out. These were young, extremely horny guys who had not seen a woman, other than pin up photos, for the better part of a year. We escorted her off the station and asked her to cover up for her own safety.

I got a little thrill of my own while we were there. We needed to work the buoys in the small boat channel, but the ship drew too much water to get into the channel. So, the skipper asked for volunteers to dive down and check the buoys shackles and anchors.

A seaman named Stafford and I volunteered. I had done a lot of diving, both free diving and SCUBA. We had no tanks on the ship so it was going to be a free dive.

I had just made a dive and was surfacing next to the small boat when I felt a turbulence in the water and saw a gray shadow. People who witnessed this said it looked like I had been shot out of the water by a cannon. I don't think I even touched the gunwale of the boat as I entered it. It's a wonder what adrenaline can do for you. When I looked back over the transom, there was a curious monk seal looking back at me. After I rinsed out my trunks, we finished our dive and then used the small boat to tow a couple of buoys we had selected back to the ship. The buoys were serviced and then put back on station.

I was able to do a couple of dives for myself while we were at French Frigate. It was fantastic. The water was crystal clear and the kinds of coral were numerous and healthy. There were brain corals, dish corals, and fan corals in wonderful colors. The sea life was beyond belief, indescribable in numbers and species. They were all around me, and some were as curious about me as I was about them. One little guy came up and put his nose right against my facemask and looked in at me. He was probably wondering what the heck kind of a creature I was, and what I was doing in his neighborhood.

This nature stuff was not Gun's cup of tea. He stayed aboard, except in Guam where he could get a drink. Well, it had been an interesting trip, but we were all ready to get back to Hono and have a little fun on liberty. As it turned out, it was going to be some of our last liberty in Hawaii.

8 ROTATIONS AND PROMOTIONS

When we returned from the Bird Watcher Patrol, we found several of our new crewmembers waiting on the dock. Several of our old ones were packed and ready to go to their next duty assignments. Our new XO and warrant bosun reported aboard and one of our most colorful crewmembers left. I did not serve with him long, but he left an indelible impression on all who he came in contact with.

Chief boatswain's mate Rob Roy McGarrity was about 5 foot 4 inches tall and would weigh maybe 140 pounds if he were wearing a wet pea coat. The only part of a chief's uniform he wore while working was a khaki chief's hat and a khaki belt. Other than that, he wore dungarees just like the rest of the crew. He was one tough little S.O.B., and there was nobody on the crew who did not, for damned sure, know who the chief of the boat was.

The chief smoked these big green cigars that smelled terrible.

One of his meaner habits was to wait until we were underway, then when he spotted a new crewmember looking a little green around the gills, he would walk up and blow smoke in his face. He got a big chuckle watching them run for the ships rail, then barf over the side. Of course, one guy barfing had a domino effect on other crewmembers and you sometimes had a whole row of guys at the rail.

Don't get me wrong. The chief loved his guys and he took care of them. He would get in the face of anybody on the ship, officer or enlisted alike, in the defense of his deck force. If the chief saw one of his men hanging around the ship during off duty hours while in port, he would tell him to either go on liberty or break out his correspondence course and study. That, or the chief would sit down and teach the kid something from his vast knowledge of seamanship. Chief McGarrity certainly knew his way around a buoy deck, and he was going to be missed for his know-how, if not for his personality.

I knew we were going to miss him at our Judo classes over on the windward side of the island. The chief, his son, three other guys, and I had discovered a traditional Judo dojo sitting near the top of the mountain, looking down on Kaneohe and the North Shore and the Pacific Ocean beyond. We were the only Caucasians in an old-style school. The *sensei* was in his nineties and two of his sons were Black Belt instructors. Everything in the place was from Japan, including the sliding panel walls and the mats. The chief was forty-four at the time and working on his Brown Belt. Well, we were all going to be gone soon, but it had been a fun six months as well as good exercise.

30

The New Warrant Bosun, Frank Souza, was a W-3. He was Portuguese and from Hawaii.

Souza came in the Coast Guard the same year I was born and was definitely old school. This was going to present a conflict problem in the future. The person who was to be our new chief boatswain's mate, was already aboard and was being promoted from BM1 to chief. His name was John Paneira. He was also Portuguese and from Hawaii and he was new school, a totally modern boatswain's mate. And he would be working for the warrant. I guess you can get the drift.

There were a couple of notable things about the new warrant bosun. He had a very interesting collection of body art, which included pigs on the calves of both legs. And the fact that he could remember every dirty joke he had ever heard. He kept us in stitches during those long night watches up on the bridge while we were in Vietnam.

Our new XO was a Lieutenant named Dan Young. He was a nice guy, but kind of quiet and reserved, which was good for me, because as much as I had a boss, he was it. The independent duty corpsmen on Coast Guard ships always reported to the XO. This meant as long as we did our jobs, no one messed with us.

Along with all this crew movement, there was also scuttlebutt (gossip) going around about our home port being changed to Guam in the Mariana Islands, a long WESTPAC, and the possibility of duty in Vietnam. Well, we were all excited by this. It was all anyone could talk about while sitting around whatever bar we were drinking in. As you might imagine, there was a lot of speculation. Where exactly, would we be going and what were we going to do in Vietnam? One of the other buoy tenders from Honolulu, the *Planetree* had already departed for Vietnam the previous month.

The only other topic was promotions. The list for June 15th promotions had been posted and Guns and I, as well as several other crewmembers, were on it. That meant that very shortly we would be getting our asses tossed over the side of the ship. This was something that happened whenever anyone got promoted, another one of our rowdy shipboard traditions. That wetting down would be followed by another kind of wetting down, usually at the EM Club, and drinks were on those who were promoted.

Being a petty officer first class on a buoy tender was pretty hot shit. In many cases, you were the senior or only person in your area of expertise. It meant you and your fellow first class had your own table on the mess deck and ate before the lower ranks. Petty officers first class also had their own berthing area and no longer had to sleep in the zoo (crew's berthing). In my case, as the ship's corpsman, I slept in the sick bay, but now if I had patients, I had a bunk in the first class quarters.

The promotion hoopla culminated, as I said, with throwing those over the side who had been promoted. This required chasing them down, in some cases. There was one young seaman who really got off on this. He wasn't on the ship long, but he managed to become a minor legend while he was there. This kid was about average height but he was built like a pencil. He had a fuzz of blonde hair and a big goofy smile. We all called him Lurch. I don't know if many people knew his real name.

He had to be hyperactive or something, because he never quit moving. When they were throwing the promoted guys over the side, he would get really excited, pace back and forth and jump up and down.

He would clap his hands while yelling, "yeah, yeah, throw them over, throw them over" like some kind of crazy person. Each time when the crew had run out of promoted guys, they always grabbed Lurch and threw him over the side just for the hell of it.

Lurch became infamous for one other thing. He was the source of the "Shit Torpedo." At chow time, this guy would fill his plate to heaping. Some said he would go back for seconds and even thirds. He never gained a pound, but when he went to the head, he created feces the size of small boat fenders. Occasionally, he even plugged the head and that was hard to do with the ship's high pressure commodes that flushed directly to the sea. The damage control man, our onboard plumber, hated him.

This talent became generally known to the crew one day when another other seamen was looking out the porthole of the crew's head (who knows why) and that's when he saw it. An eighteen-inch turd flew from the outlet pipe that ran just below the shitters and came out of the hull about three feet above the ship's waterline. It flew about three or four feet and splashed into the water. The crewman hollered at the top of his lungs "Jesus Christ, a shit torpedo."

Well, the word of this miracle buzzed around the crews berthing area. Lurch became a household name in the forecastle and the information about his amazing ability was stored away in a bunch of fertile but devious minds for future reference.

Soon after the promotions were over, our new skipper arrived. His name was Robert Slater. He was a lieutenant commander who had been a first class quartermaster before going to OCS. He was probably about five feet nine inches tall with dark brown hair cut short and speckled with a little gray. He had blue eyes and an easy smile.

Being an ex-white hat (enlisted) he was a sailor's skipper and had no problem empathizing with the enlisted crewmen. This would be

Captain Slater's first command at sea. Since leaving OCS fifteen years earlier, he had seen mostly shore duty.

Our new Engineering Officer, CWO2 Ralph Gilbert, reported aboard about the same time as the skipper. Mr. Gilbert and the skipper seemed to hit it off right away and they would become good friends. This friendship caused some talk, as well as some crude remarks in the ranks, and would eventually result in a preemptive strike against him with the shit torpedo.

After the change of command ceremony, the new CO took over and we finally got the official word on where we were going and some of what we would be doing. LCDR Slater also made some other announcements. We were now going to be allowed to have civilian clothes aboard. Before this, we had always had to keep them at a locker club or at the Honolulu YMCA. He said for some of the places we were going, we would be required to wear civvies on liberty.

Later that day, he had a meeting with all the first class deck ratings. He told us this was his first command at sea, that he was short of chief petty officers and he had a new XO and a brand new ensign aboard. He said we were going to some places that made him kind of nervous about the lack of experienced officers.

That's when he told us. "Gentlemen, at this point I'm going to put my faith in hash marks (service stripes). Between you, you have a lot of years in the service. Before our deployment to Vietnam, you are each going to learn what goes on up on the bridge. I want an extra set of eyes up there during underway watches in the war zone. So, I'm appointing you guys as underway JOODs. Since you'll be accepting some of the responsibilities of officers, you will be given the privileges of officers as much as possible, like open gangway in port when you don't have the watch. I'm going to be counting on you guys. Don't let me down."

That's when I made a decision. The new XO Mr. Young had been impressed with the record of my performance during our recent underway training. Then, when I made first class short of time in grade, and they needed a waiver from headquarters to promote me, he figured I was officer material. He was getting all the paperwork done to recommend me for OCS, Officer Candidate School. When I heard about some of the places we were going, I pulled my application. I had been training with and getting to know my shipmates for the past several months, and I just did not want to miss this trip that had the whole crew excited.

33

9 GETTING READY FOR OUR NEW HOME

Well, it was official. We were going to Guam and our dance card was full with an ambitious schedule of work to be done. Guam is an island about 4,000 miles from Hawaii. We had three stops along the way before we arrived at our new home port in Apra Harbor. Cruising at nine knots and counting our stops along the way, it would take us a month to reach our new home. We would be there just three days and off again to work aids to navigation on a couple of islands in the U.S. Trust Territories. After that, we would return to Guam for a few days and then be off again.

At some point, we would be doing some work in Vietnam. First would be a logistics run to bring supplies from the Army Supply Depot in Sattahip, Thailand over to our people at the Coast Guard LORAN Station on Con Son Island, Vietnam. That would be followed by three or four months of work on navigation aids up and down the coast and in the rivers and bays from the Gulf of Thailand to the DMZ.

The CO said there was also talk about something different regarding our duties in Vietnam. The Coast Guard and Navy brass were working out the details. We would not get the word on what it was until just before we arrived in country.

It seemed like everything was happening in double time and everybody, including yours truly, was running around like crazy. We were all trying to get our departments ready for the long deployment and new crewmembers were coming aboard daily, many of them from the same boot camp company.

We were increasing the crew from around fifty-five to sixty-four, in anticipation of our Vietnam deployment. This was to provide extra watch standers and to man the two additional .50 caliber machine guns we would be receiving. Time was short, so all the department heads were going from ship to ship in the harbor at Sand Island with blank requisition forms in hand looking for things we might need. I took a trip over to medical supply at Pearl Harbor to get the items I needed, things that could not wait to come through our normal supply channels.

The Coast Guard is not like the Navy. We don't travel in battle groups with carriers and destroyers and support ships. In the Navy, if you have no ketchup for your burger, no sweat, you can have a bottle choppered over from the supply ship. In the Coast Guard, we travel in small solitary ships. If you have not thought of it before you got underway, you didn't have it. Tough shit, at sea for us meant, what you see is what you've got.

34

Guns also had his work cut out for him working with the damage control man to build mounts on the fantail for the two new machine guns. The skipper also wanted chest high armor plating welded in front of all four mounts. The .50s already had shields above that.

While we were on underway training during gunnery exercises, Guns discovered one of his guns was firing out of sync. Now he needed to test fire the repaired gun and dropped by at sick bay to ask for help.

"Doc, I just finished rebuilding my fifty. I think I've got it fixed. It was missing one of the recoil baffles. There's supposed to be twenty-one of them and that gun only had twenty. Now, I've got to test fire it to make sure it's working right. The last thing we want to do is end up in a war zone with a malfunctioning machine gun. I could use your help. You want to take a ride?"

"Sure. Where are you going to fire it?"

"Let's go over to Fort Shafter and borrow a ground mount from the Army and then take it out to their range and shoot up a couple of boxes of ammo."

"Sounds like a plan. Let me lock up sick bay and tell the XO where I'm going."

We grabbed the gun and a couple of cans of ammo. We threw them in the back of an old beater government van that was used by all seven ships that called Sand Island home port. It was light gray and was covered with dents and dings. U.S. Coast Guard was painted on each side in peeling black letters. Guns and I were in faded dungaree and chambray shirts wearing *Basswood* ball caps and boondockers (high top work shoes). I wasn't even sure the Army would let us in. Back then, most of the people in the large military services didn't know what the Coast Guard was or what we did. They probably still don't.

After some dubious looks and a careful check of our ID cards, the Army gate guards supplied us with directions to the armory and passed us through the gate.

We were to contact a Major Poole. We found the armory and Major Poole and told him what we needed. He provided us with a ground mount (tripod) and gave us directions to a place we could fire our gun.

It was a large facility and after driving around for about fifteen minutes, Guns asked, "Does this look like the place?"

I said, "It looks good to me."

There was a wide spot where a number of vehicles could pull off the road and then a low fence of short white posts supporting white painted chain. In front of the chain was a smooth area of hard packed dirt about fifteen feet deep. After that, there was wide open field out for about 800 yards, right up against a thick tropical forest (jungle).

"Shit, this looks like a great spot, Doc. Let's give her a go. I'll get the gun and put it on the mount, you grab the ammo."

Guns set up the machine gun, opened a box of ammo, fed the belt into the receiver, and jacked a round home. First, he fired off some single rounds and then some short three-round bursts. Then, he went full automatic. We were just blowing the shit out of the jungle and trees, leaves and brush were flying in the air.

Guns let up on the trigger and said, "Here Doc, you take a turn."

I got behind the gun and finished up the first 104-round can of ammo.

Guns said, "No use carrying that other can of ammo back with us. Let's shoot it up."

While he was loading the gun, I heard a shrill whistling. Someone was yelling from about 100 hundred yards to the right of our position and way out in the field.

Then I saw a soldier in camouflage battle dress. He had a big red stripe on his helmet. He came out of the jungle on his belly and he was screaming, "Cease fire! Cease fire!"

Then, he jumped up and double-timed over to where we were standing.

"Who the fuck are you people? What are you doing firing that damned machine gun here? We've got people out there doing field exercises."

We told him who we were and what we were doing.

Guns said, "We were told by Major Poole that it would be okay to test fire our gun here."

"That fucking idiot Poole! He should have known we would be out here today."

"No one was injured, were they?" Guns asked.

The sergeant said, "No, but it was just good luck that we were not right in front of you guys."

"We're sure sorry we shot up your war games, sergeant. We've done what we come to do. We'll take off now and you can get back to your training. And you might want to give the major another heads up."

The soldier did an about face and stomped off back to his troops, cussing all the way. I'm not sure, but I think I heard something in his tirade that sounded like, "Fucking Coast Guard."

As we drove back to Sand Island, we were pretty quiet with our own thoughts about what could have been. We cleaned the gun and stowed it, then hit the rain locker, and got cleaned up just in time to make happy hour at the EM Club. Another day's work in the U.S. Coast Guard was done.

After getting a few Happy Hour drinks in him, Guns was taking credit for improving the quality of Army training by providing those grunts in the field exercise some live fire experience.

10 LEAVING HAWAII

These were definitely exciting times, but bittersweet. We were all going to miss our time in Hawaii and the friends we had made. I was going to miss many things, including sitting with Cho Sin on the lawn near the beach outside the Queen Surf on the Diamond Head end of Waikiki Beach. We would often sit there listening to Hawaiian music and watching the magnificent sunsets out over the sea. My forays over to the undeveloped North Shore and out into the neighborhoods visiting with the locals, I would miss it all, but only for a little while.

When they threw the mooring lines off of the *Basswood* and we got underway, my mind would be soaring ahead of us anticipating new sights and new sounds and new smells and new adventures. God, it was good to be young and single and a sailor.

I don't think many of us knew that we were about to embark on a fifteen-month odyssey across the Pacific and would experience some of the most memorable times of our lives. We would go to islands so remote that we had to draw them in on our charts.

Places the National Geographic had not been. We would meet Micronesian islanders on small atolls so far off the beaten path that they still lived much like they had hundreds of years ago.

Well, the day finally arrived on the 17th of August 1967. We were on our way. Next stop was Johnston Island, which was a restricted island and part of the Pacific Missile Range. After that it would be the 180th Parallel (The International Date Line). It would be my first time across and I had trepidations about things I'd heard about the crossing initiation. With each rumor it got worse. It didn't sound like a lot of fun, at least not for us pollywogs.

Leaving for the last time was a big deal. There were dignitaries on the pier, as well as crew family members. There were speeches. There was Hawaiian music and there were hula dancers on the fantail and we all got flower Leis. I was wearing tropical whites and flat hat with a pink lei around my neck standing at my fantail phone talker, sea detail ready for getting underway.

The hula girls took one last pass around the fantail. They passed the quarterdeck and danced down the gangway. The gangway was hauled aboard. All the mooring lines were taken in except number two, the spring line. When the ship moved away from the dock, number two was taken in. At the same time, the boson's pipe was sounded and the colors were simultaneously lowered on the flagstaff aft and raised on the main mast. We were underway.

We passed the sea buoy and secured special sea detail. The crew shifted into their work uniforms and waited for the abandon ship drill. This was usually done when first getting underway on a trip, particularly with so many new hands aboard. Everybody needed to know where to go and how to abandon ship in an emergency.

After that, everyone went back to their assigned stations and underway work details.

When you're a Coast Guard Sailor, you have to become one with the sea or you're going to be an unhappy camper. This is particularly true when you are going to sea in a very small ship like the *Basswood*. She was a very lively lady, and it did not take much of a sea to provide a lot of motion. Due to her shape and ice breaker bow, she would ride up and crash through the oncoming sea swells and then roll from side to side on the way down the back of the swell. The next thirty days would test the new guys and they would find out if they were suited to life aboard a small Coast Guard ship. If they couldn't hack it, couldn't get past the sea sickness, I would have to get them transferred to shore duty. Since everyone was expected to be qualified for sea duty, that would essentially end their Coast Guard careers.

I was one of the lucky ones. I loved it when we were at sea, the rougher the better. I never even had a hint of sea sickness. My food tasted better. I even slept better, albeit there were times that I had to tie myself in my bunk to do it. I felt the motion of the decks under my feet. I inhaled the air, a combination of the sea breeze, the stack gas from the diesel engines, and the noon meal cooking in the galley. It was wonderful and all was right with my world.

I looked back wistfully one last time as Oahu became smaller and smaller. Then I turned around and walked forward between the port life boat and the deck house. I leaned on the forward rail above the buoy deck and looked towards the horizon. I thought to myself *'What's out there? What kinds of things am I going to see?'* Well, the next adventure was going to be crossing the 180 in eleven days after a short stop at Johnston Island.

11 ENTERING THE REALM

Well, the seas were kind. When we left Hawaii, they were running about two feet, which is really nothing. By the next day they were almost flat calm. That was okay with us because we knew that in the months ahead, we were bound to face some of the roughest seas the Pacific could throw at us.

Our first stop would be Johnston Island, which was precisely in the middle of nowhere, half-way between Hawaii and the 180th meridian. It was part of the Pacific Missile Range. There were no locals on this island, only some military and a bunch of civilian contractors. Oh, and a Coast Guard Loran "A" Station. There was a Loran "A" station on almost every rock in the Pacific big enough to build one on.

Loran "A" had been around since the end of WWII. In spite of its name, "Long Range", it was in reality, fairly short range. That's why they needed so many of them. Loran "A" would soon be replaced by the longer range and more accurate Loran "C" Stations.

We were carrying some supplies for this station and that was one of the reasons for stopping. That and to let the crew get off the boat for a little R & R, very little as it turned out.

We all had to have a security clearance to even get ashore. Well, the workers at Johnston had all the creature comforts and recreation equipment to make their eighteen-month stays a little kinder. They had a real movie theater and an un-staffed casino with craps tables and blackjack tables and slot machines. It was the kind of casino where you supplied your own dealers. They also had a nice bar with food available, a bowling alley, and many other perks. There were all sorts of tradesmen and technicians stationed there. If they signed on for the full eighteen months, they paid no U.S. income taxes and received a bonus when they finished their tour.

If there were any women around, they must have hidden them, because we didn't see any. That meant Guns and I had to find other ways to amuse ourselves. This is when I found out my buddy Guns Gunderson could sing.

"What do you know about this place, Guns?"

"I know that the workers make big bucks and don't have anywhere to spend it. I also know that they are lonely and like to visit with anyone who feels a little like back home. And finally, my good friend Doc, I know that we aren't going to pay for a single drink."

That's when he hauled out his concertina. "What's the hell is that?" I asked.

40

"Come on, you'll see."

He was right, we didn't pay for anything. He threw his hat on the bar, broke out the concertina, and commenced to sing and play every sailor song and sea chantey anyone had ever heard, as well as many old favorite popular songs.

Sometimes, he would even dance a little sailor's hornpipe jig while he played. Guns Gunderson was one hell of a guy to have as a liberty buddy. When we left, not only had we not paid for anything, there was also a couple hundred bucks in the white hat he had left on the bar. Being the good buddies that we were, he split the take with me.

Well, one day was enough of Johnston Island and the next morning we were off, with the dreaded crossing initiation looming over my head. The Guns was not sweating it. He had been across many times. He was also not telling me shit about what to expect, like why the golden dragons were saving all the ships' wet garbage in cans, up in the forecastle.

A week before we were due to arrive at the dateline, they declared Hell Week open. This is where the pollywogs have a chance to get even with the golden dragons for the shit they were going to rain down on us on initiation day.

Except for the captain, I was the senior pollywog. Although the CO would go through the initiation, he could not be a party to the shenanigans the pollywogs would pull on the dragons. That left it to me to lead the insurrection. I had a few tricks up my sleeve. The first thing we tried failed. We spotted a group of golden dragons sitting out on the fantail one day. They were the planning committee for the 180 ceremony.

A group of us unrolled a three-inch fire hose and charged it. We were creeping up on the dragons and when we got close enough, I pulled the handle on the nozzle and just a couple of drips came out. Then we heard a loud voice behind us and we all knew who it was. Joe Sherman, was a giant first class boatswain's mate from Maine. He was about six-foot-six and I could not weigh him because my sick bay scale only went to 350 pounds.

He had that fire hose bent in half and crimped in his hands like it was a God-damned little garden hose.

He hollered, "Okay, you slimy pollywogs, turn off that fire hose and secure it back where you found it."

And we did. Okay dragons, I thought, *You win this round, but we've got more.*

My next gag was the best of all of them. Only a corpsman could have pulled this one off. In my lab gear, I had different types of powdered tissue dyes that were used to do microscopic tests. The dyes reacted with the organisms you were looking for, through the scope, and became visible. These dyes also reacted with water.

In the crew's head, there were two paper towel dispensers. I took the towels out of one and sprinkled the powdered dye in the folds of the towels and then returned them to the dispenser. Then, I told all the pollywogs to only use the other one. It took about six dragons to figure it out, but by then it was too late for them. They would come in from work heading for chow. They would make a pit stop at the head, then wash their hands and usually their faces. We were in the tropics after all, and they were hot and sweaty. When the dye powder reacted with the water on their hands and faces, it left stains like those big strawberry birthmarks you see on some people. Oh, and it could not be washed off. It had to wear off. There were more tricks that were pulled on the golden dragons, but no need to dwell on them here. By the time initiation day rolled around, needless to say, they were pretty pissed at me.

We arrived at the 180th meridian at 13.30 north latitude on 26 August. The first thing the golden dragons did was round us pollywogs up. Then, they gave us screwed up haircuts.

They'd take a chunk out here and there, but often it could be repaired by a barber. If you gave them a reason, they would really fuck it up.

Once again, being the smart ass, I put pure lanolin/wool fat in my hair. That shit was like really thick vaseline. It was very sticky. To that I added table salt and combed it all in. They took one swipe with the electric clippers, and they were shot. Not to be deterred, they hauled out a set of manual clippers and messed up my hair so bad I had to shave my head.

After the haircuts, you are striped to your skivvies and herded up to the fantail. While we had been getting our haircuts, the dragons had been preparing the site and getting dressed in costumes made from whatever they could find aboard ship. Some were quite creative.

Then, they held a Kangaroo Court back on the fantail where they would read the charges against you. These charges were designed to be insulting and were made up from anything personal they could find out or make up about you. Again, your punishment depended on your attitude.

They asked me how I pled. I said "not guilty", then turned around and bent over. Across the ass of my skivvies was written "Golden Dragon's Open Mess." For that, I got thirty lashes with an old piece of fire hose. I might add here that Gun's job as master-at-arms during the proceedings was to make sure things did not get out of hand.

I'm sure you're wondering by now what all this silly shit is about. As far as I've been able to find out, it came from the early days of the British Navy during England's empire-building days when British war ships spanned the globe. It was used as a morale booster, of all things, to raise the spirit of crews faced with the hardships of shipboard life and endless months at sea.

At some point, these ceremonies became traditions and were eventually passed on to the American Navy as well. There are now many such ceremonies for various crossings around the globe, but the two oldest are for the equator and the International Date Line. (180th Parallel)

As our sentences were handed down, and after we received our lashes, we were lined up in the starboard air castle at the top of the ladder overlooking the buoy deck. That's when I found out what the garbage was for. Some of the boatswain's mate dragons had created a long tube made of canvas, and you guessed it, it was filled with about two weeks-worth of the ship's slop garbage that had been fermenting in the heat of the forecastle.

On each side of the tube was a line of golden dragons in colorful makeshift costumes and armed with sections of old fire hose. One end of the tube started at the bottom of the ladder where we were standing, and the other end came out near the Royal Court which consisted of the Royal Baby, the Queen, and the King. It was quite a sight to behold.

We entered the tube and crawled on our bellies through the vile, stinking mess it contained. We were continually pummeled by the gauntlet of dragons lined up along the tube. At the other end, we had to do honor to the Royal Court.

First, you were to kiss the royal baby's stomach. The royal baby in this case was one of the Filipino stewards. I think they picked him because of his great big Buddha belly. He was wearing only a diaper which smelled very much like it might have been soiled, but who could tell after the experience in the tube? He had his belly all greased up with something slimy and foul smelling. We were on our knees at this point and I bent forward to kiss his belly. As I did, he grabbed my head and rubbed my face all around in whatever he had smeared on his stomach.

The next stop was at the Queen, where you were to kiss the Royal Snatch. The guy playing the Queen was my table mate at the first class chow table. He was a first class electronics technician named Bender. Bender was a kind of skinny guy with black hair and a big mouth, both figuratively and literally. He was okay as a guy, but he made one fucking ugly woman. He was wearing a wig made from a swab head

43

(mop head) and was wearing a makeshift skirt that was hiked up to his waist. His legs were spread apart, and he had a large sponge strapped to his groin. It was smeared with ketchup and sardines and anything else nasty he could think of. He pulled the same thing the baby did by pushing your face right into the Royal Snatch.

Next and last was King Neptune, who was played by the warrant bosun wearing a great big crown made of heavy duty tin foil. The King read the creed and pronounced that we had now been found worthy to be Golden Dragons. He then ordered swim call to commence. The deck crew hung a cargo net over the side of the ship, posted sharp shooters on the bridge wing and on top of the forecastle, and swim call started with us diving into the Pacific to wash the nasty grime off of our bodies. So, for all intents and purposes, we swam across the 180. Not many people can say that, because you can't do things like that on large ships.

When swim call was over the ship was hosed down and cleaned and the 55-gallon drum barbeque pit was set up. While I enjoyed my ration of two beers the former Royal Baby cooked me one of the best tasting steaks I ever ate. Only in the Coast Guard!

12 KWAJALEIN AND ENIEWETOK

Underway as before, we were on the way to Kwajalein Atoll, located 2,100 nautical miles southwest of Honolulu and half way to Guam. We had another two weeks of steaming time until we reached that destination, but the seas continued to be almost flat and the weather was beautiful. So, it was back to killing time for the crew.

The new Chief Bosun's Mate John Paneira kept the deck force occupied with busy work. There was always something that needed to be painted on a ship. Below decks, the engine room crew serviced the mechanical gear and kept everything running smoothly. Even with this, and watch standing, there is still a lot of dead time at sea.

On the *Basswood*, there was not a lot of room to do anything except exist. Only about 40 feet of the 180-foot vessel was dedicated to crew space for the sixty-four man crew to eat, clean up, and sleep. The ship had no air conditioning and except for the few places with portholes, the interior of the ship was airless and hot.

Forty sweating men were jammed into the crews berthing area, which was below decks and provided hardly enough room to turn around. The men who inhabited this space for the most part did hard dirty work and the place reeked of sweaty body odor. It didn't help matters that the ship did not make its own potable water.

This meant that when we were a long distance from a place where we could take on water, the crew took sea showers. Sea showers are short, only three minutes, and there was a bosun standing by with a stop watch to make sure you used only your allotted time. You would turn the water on just long enough to get wet and then turn it off. Next, you would soap down and wash. After that, you would turn on the water just long enough to rinse off. Unless you did really dirty work, you were not allowed to shower every day.

The crew did a variety of things to entertain themselves. They read books from the supply of paperbacks onboard, played board games on the tables on the mess deck, or played cards. We only had two chiefs aboard, and one of them was a poker player. The chief's mess was turned into a poker parlor and except for meal times, there was a non-stop game going the whole time we were underway. When one guy went on watch, another guy coming off watch would take his spot at the table.

The two biggest morale factors for the crew were the evening movies and chow. In good weather, the movies were shown out on the fantail. My reserved seat for the movies was one arm of the towing bit. The meals served by CS2 Bobby Green were the best I'd ever eaten in the Coast Guard. He should have been a chief petty officer, but he was another one of the guys who did not test well.

Some people still bitched. Being a cook was a thankless job. No matter what you served, you couldn't cook like everybody's mom.

I got to know Bobby pretty well since the door to the galley was right across the passageway from the sick bay. We used to talk when it was slow in the galley. He was a solitary guy, a loner. Everybody called him the Merchie, because of his liberty clothes, I suppose. He wore short sleeve cotton sport shirts buttoned up to the neck, khaki chinos, and dessert boots all topped off with a snap brim straw hat with a little feather in the hat band. He usually went off by himself. Besides being a great cook, he was a talented marine artist. He could draw boats and ships that were so realistic it looked as if you could have gone aboard and sailed away in them.

Bobby's other nickname was Mr. Clean. He wore his hair cut right to the scalp and he was fastidious about cleanliness. Probably as obsessive-compulsive as you could be aboard a Coast Guard ship. He hated having to live in the zoo with the lower-rated animals.

I remember one day when he came to sick bay horrified. He had found a crab louse on his body. I checked out the other guys that slept in the same stack of racks as Bobby and came up with a third class petty officer who must have been the shipboard distributer for crabs. He was crawling with them. If they had been allowed to go on much longer, I think his dick would have dropped off.

One other thing that the cook confided to me was another practice that went on down in crew berthing.

"You know Doc," he said. "I don't mind it so much when the guys jack off in their socks, but darn it (he didn't swear), I really hate it when they use my socks."

Evidently, someone had found Green's clean socks, stuffed in is boondockers (work shoes). The guy did his business and returned the socks when he was finished, only to be discovered by the cook as he slipped them on the next morning.

Finally, Kwajalein came up on the horizon. We were not expecting much there in the way of liberty, and we were right. It was probably going to be another night drinking with Guns playing the concertina. And that's what it turned out to be.

There were some interesting things about Kwajalein from a purely educational point of view. With ninety-seven islands or islets and a total length of 175 miles enclosing a lagoon with an area of 1,100 square miles, it was the largest coral atoll in the world. The island of Kwajalein was the largest and that's where we were going. There were maybe ten or twelve thousand people scattered around the atoll, but less than a thousand lived on Kwajalein and those were mostly American government workers and some U.S. Army personnel.

We spent the night and sailed across the lagoon on the way out the next morning. The lagoon teemed with sea life. You could see them below the surface of the clear water, and fish jumped in the air as the ship passed. The next morning, we were back out on the open ocean and bound for Eniewetok Atoll.

After sick call, I spent a lot of my time up on deck. You could usually find me standing in the forward part of the port air castle leaning on the rail and watching the horizon.

If not there, I would be sitting on one of the benches on the fantail having a smoke, drinking coffee, and shooting the shit with whoever else was out there. You would find me in these places at sunrise and sunset for sure. I have never seen such glorious sunrises or sunsets as I have on the open ocean. They are just one more of God's indescribable rewards for being a sailor.

Eniewetok has 40 islands and was another bastion of government interest over the years. After the end of WWII the inhabitants, who had already suffered under Japanese occupation, were further traumatized by being forced to evacuate their home islands so the U.S. could conduct nuclear tests there. Think Bikini Island, from 1948 to 1954. The United States did 43 nuclear tests there including the first hydrogen bomb. The islands that were involved and those located nearby, we were told, would not be safe for human habitation until sometime in the late seventies or eighties. Hey, there was a bar near where we moored. Nobody glowed in the dark, so all was well.

The next day we were back at sea and on to our new home on Guam.

13 GUAM IS GOOD, NOT!

We arrived at Apra Harbor in Agana Guam on 10 September 1967 and were escorted to our dock space by fire boats spraying their water cannons. There were a few dignitaries and senior officers from the USCG MARSEC (Marianas Section) office waiting, but not as much hoopla as when we left Hawaii. Also waiting on the dock were some new crewmembers. A few men transferred off and went on to other assignments. This included the infamous Lurch.

Our skipper's first official act was to pull rank on the junior captains of the Navy ships tied up in the harbor and take the best mooring site in the harbor for the *Basswood*.

We were only going to be in port three days so we did not get much of a chance to look around. First, the Guns and I went over to the Navy Base EM Club for a drink. It was noisy and crowded. "Light My Fire" by the Doors was cranked up on the juke box.

"Look at this fucking place, Guns. How many squids you think are here, 500, 600?"

"Too fucking many, let's have one drink and then go downtown."

We had nothing against the Navy guys. They could not help being institutionalized by life in such a large service. We called a cab and went to town. The cab ride cost us $15.00 one way and when we arrived there was nothing much there. We had a drink at a Filipino Pancitaria/Bar where a fat old Filipina served us a very expensive beer while we were forced to listen to Pilita Corales' rendition of "Dahil sayo."

We were pretty despondent when we returned to the ship that day. The next day we discovered the Merchant Marine Bar just a short walk from where we were tied up. We spent the next two days drinking there until we got underway again.

We had both heard rumors about Guam and they were not good.

"Yeah, well how could it not be? It's 30 miles long and 12 miles wide and it's overrun with military."

"What have we got," Guns said. "Let's see, there's the big Anderson Air Force Base flying B-52 bombers to Vietnam on one end of the island. Then we have a couple of Navy Bases, not counting the nuclear sub base across the harbor on this end. Even the Coast Guard has a pretty big footprint here with the Coast Guard Air Station and Section Office, a LORAN Station, the Buoy Depot, and now us."

"And don't forget Guns, there are seventy thousand or so Chamorros (Guamanians) stuck in the middle trying to earn a living and keep their women away from a bunch of horny service guys."

"Well, Doc, I think the best thing about Guam is going to be the fact that we're not going to be here much."

"Amen buddy.

"And the good news," Guns said, "is we're leaving in the morning."

"Truk Island and Ponape, those are new ones for me, Doc. Maybe we will be able to test the big fish theory with that tuna you caught. See if it can catch us a couple of them little native girls. You should have the cooks move it to the chill box to thaw. Just in case the fish doesn't work, we should probably bring a couple of cans of Spam with us."

Spam had come to the Pacific with the G.I.'s of WWII and had since become a delicacy almost everywhere we went, from Hawaii to the Philippines and all the islands in between. It had been adapted to all kinds of native recipes and some were quite good.

14 INTO THE TRUST TERRITORIES

So, you're probably wondering about the Trust Territories of the Pacific. I'll try not to get bogged down in this and give you the quick version. The Trust Territories consists of several groups of islands in the Western Pacific. They include the Marshall, the Mariana Islands, and the Caroline Islands which include the Yap group and the Palau Islands. Truk and Ponape are part of the Carolines and are located roughly in the center of the Trust Territories.

These islands were discovered by the Spaniards in the 1500s. They were later sold to the Germans who owned them up until the end of the First World War. The Japanese occupied many of them before and during WWII. After the war, the Americans took over the islands and established the Trust Territories and would eventually give them autonomy and self rule within their individual island groups. Our first trip was going to be to Truk and Ponape, both fairly large islands, but sparsely populated.

Truk was an important Japanese Naval Headquarters and supply depot for their Pacific Fleet during WWII. Now it has a small harbor facility and town. What economy there was came from the government administrators and their staff and the sale of copra (dried coconut meat). Most of the natives on the island live a subsistence lifestyle and use the barter system to provide their basic needs. We would be in Truk a couple of days working aids to navigation in the area.

Now, I don't want you to think we just popped over to these islands. It usually involved from three to several days at sea sailing between islands. We had just sailed from Guam into Truk Lagoon after a little over three days at sea. There was a large supply barge tied up to the pier, so we would be dropping anchor and going ashore in the ship's small boats. It was mid-day, so liberty was granted. We would work the local aids to navigation in the morning.

Guns and I were out on the fantail having a smoke. It was steak day and we were going to wait and have chow on the ship before we caught the liberty boat to town. While we were out there, I noticed the skipper and Mr. Gilbert motoring off in the captain's gig and I gave a little chuckle.

"What are you laughing at Doc?"

"I was just thinking back to Lurch and the Shit Torpedo."

"Oh yeah, that was funny."

Lurch was gone now, transferred off when we arrived in Guam, but he had been able to fulfill his destiny on the way over.

The skipper and the EO Mr. Gilbert had become tight during the first couple of months they were aboard.

To me and the rest of the non-coms, they were just buddies. Everyone needs a friend, even the captain. Being the CO of a ship is a very lonely job.

Well, to the young non-rates aboard, this smacked of ass-kissing on the part of the EO. These seamen are the on board worker bees who did the hard work and got all the shit jobs. So, they were always bitching about something. It's been that way as long as ships have been going to sea. To the deck hands in the forecastle, ass-kissing was a mortal sin.

Now, even I had to admit that Mr. Gilbert was not your typical engineering officer. Most of the engineers I had come across in my years in the service were a little rough around the edges, rumpled, sweaty, and grease stained. The engine room was in the bowels of the ship and the work was hot and dirty. Even in a clean engine room like ours, you would sweat through your clothes. With machines, you always had diesel fuel, oil, and grease. You were bound to rub up against something and get a grease stain on your uniform now and again.

Not Mr. Gilbert. He always looked like a recruiting poster. He was an average-sized guy, trim, fortyish, with dark, thick, wavy, salt and pepper hair. His wash khakis were spotless with knife edge creases. And for an EO, he spent an inordinate amount of time above decks, usually in the company of the captain.

I figured he was just better at delegating authority to his subordinates than most. But not the deck hands. They would say shit like, "Look at that brown nose, always following the skipper around." And "If the skipper stopped quickly, the EO would get a broken nose." "Did you guys see how he always personally gets the captain's gig ready for him and then runs him ashore?"

Many of the places we went were small and did not have docking facilities. Sometimes, the facilities were too small and our ship would not fit or there would already be another vessel tied up at the dock. For this reason, we anchored out much of the time and went ashore in the ship's small boats. The captain had his own gig in the form of a 13-foot Boston Whaler with an outboard motor. And Mr. Gilbert did indeed see that the captain's gig was lowered over the port side. Then, he would tie off the bow line and climb down the Jacob's ladder and start the engine to make sure that it was operating okay. Then, he would shut it down and sit and wait for the captain. Usually, the boat would drift back until it reached the end of the slack in the line and it would rest against the port side of the ship.

Nobody knows or will admit whether what took place when we were anchored off Eniwetok was by design or just providence. Everything came together at the right time and in the right place. But, we all had our suspicions.

It was the same drill, and Mr. Gilbert was sitting in the gig in his perfectly pressed uniform patiently waiting for the skipper. The boat had drifted back like it usually did, but a little bit further aft. It was just under the drain pipe, or scupper, from the crew's head. At the very same moment, Lurch was just finishing his business on the outboard crapper. He wiped, stood up, and "Fired the Torpedo." That is, he flushed the john.

A huge turd launched out of the side of the ship. It flew out a couple of feet where it seemed to hover, before dropping right in Mr. Gilbert's lap. Many crewmembers heard his scream and rushed to the port rail to see what the matter was. They all had to back up a step and turn around before breaking out in riotous laughter.

One crewman ran back to the fantail where Guns and I were enjoying a cup of coffee and told us what had happened. In retrospect, I thought it was a pretty awful thing that happened to Mr. Gilbert, but at the time, I almost choked and coffee sprayed out of my nose. Guns laughed so hard, he fell off of the bench. Hey, there's a lot of slack time aboard ship so you have to use it up somehow.

We had finished up noon chow and Bobby Green had out done himself again with surf and turf (steak and lobster tails). Now Guns and I were ready to hit the beach and see what there was to do on Truk. And yep, we had the 70-pound tuna as well as a few cans of Spam. Of course, with a coast guard ship anchored in the harbor, a group of curious locals had gathered at the waterfront. When we hauled that fish up on the dock, it caused quite a stir. Folks gathered around. The gunner's mate was busy negotiating, seeing what could be arranged with the fish. I think they settled on an impromptu Luau for that evening, where girls would be available for whatever you could work out.

While I was standing at the fringe of the crowd watching the proceedings, I felt a hand rubbing my arm. I looked down and there was a native girl, maybe 19 or 20 years old. She smiled up at me and giggled, and then led me away. She took me down a path through the jungle to her home, a two-room native thatched hut, where I presented her delighted mother with two cans of Spam. The girl's name, by the way, was the native equivalent of "tuna", thus the irony of it all. She took me to one of the two rooms where we spent most of the afternoon and that night. Her brother slept lying across the doorway, so no one would disturb us.

52

I decided right away that I could get to like this part of the world.

No long philosophical conversations. Verbal communications were minimal and conducted in a combination patois of the local dialect, pidgin, and a smattering of English words and giggles. Most communications were non-verbal or tactile, touch, body language, smiles, and eye expression. There was nothing tawdry about my relations with this island girl, it just felt natural. These were happy communal people who were used to sharing what they had; food, shelter and even their women.

This was not unlike the primitive Eskimo culture in the American and Canadian Arctic. Except the Pacific island girls smelled much better. The Micronesian women, I found to be very clean, and they use a lot of coconut oils on their skin and in their hair. Sleeping with them was kind of like bedding down next to a soft, smooth coconut macaroon.

The next morning, when I returned to the ship, Guns asked, "Where the hell did you disappear to?"

"You wouldn't believe me if I told you."

"Sure I would, but you missed a great time. We ate with the locals and most of us paired up with a girl and went off to various places to conclude our business."

So, I related my story to Guns. "And before I left, her mother fixed me breakfast with some of the Spam I'd given her."

"Damn," Guns said, "is this a great part of the world or what? It reminds me of that story *Mutiny on the Bounty*."

"And we have a bunch more of these islands to visit." I responded.

We worked the aids around the island that day.

We got done early and the skipper granted early liberty so we got a chance to do some exploring. Most of the infrastructure on the island; roads, light houses, and the air strip, were built by the Japanese both before and during the war. There were many old bullet-cratered concrete bunkers and storage buildings. We got a chance to snorkel in the lagoon. The lagoon had been used as a Japanese sea plane base during the war and you could see a sunken plane with the red meat ball wing markings still visible. All in all, it was a great visit.

We waved goodbye to our new friends as we left Truk, bound for Ponape. It would take us two or two and a half days to reach Ponape. Lieutenant Wyman had the watch on the bridge.

LT Brad Wyman was a reserve officer who was already aboard when I reported to the *Basswood*. LT Wyman was very tall, probably the tallest person on the ship, and very thin. He was all arms and legs and he had a very wide mouth. When he grinned, which was often, it went from ear to ear. He was also a head knocker, and his attempts to save his head had made him appear a bit clumsy. When you're as tall as Mr. Wyman, who had to really bend down to go through doors and hatches while still trying to keep his balance on a ship pitching and rolling, it was no wonder.

Mr. Wyman was our navigation officer. The quartermasters joked that they wouldn't give him the good sextant because they were afraid he would drop it and break it. Then, we would no longer be able to plot our course. These guys would also mess with his head up on the bridge, literally. Mr. Wyman's domain on the bridge was the chart table, which was located in the aft starboard corner.

This is where he would plot the ship course and keep track of our position. There was a porthole right next to the starboard side of the table. Portholes have a solid steel battle cover that can be fastened down over the glass when in combat conditions or you are running a darkened ship at night, as we had in Vietnam. That cover would normally be latched open by a brass hook.

This cover, as it turns out, was right where Mr. Wyman's head would need to be when he bent over the table. For this reason, the first thing he did when he reported to the bridge was unhook the battle cover so it would be out of his way. Then, he would go about his work checking the gyro-compass, the radar, and taking the numbers from the LORAN transmitter.

While he was doing this, one of the quartermasters hooked the battle port back up. When Mr. Wyman turned back to his table to do his calculations, you guessed it, BANG, right in the old gourd. It was an accident the first time, but it was so much fun, they started doing it every day. One other problem the LT had with his head occurred every day at Officer's Call to Quarters, which happens right after the noon meal.

Quarters are held out on the fantail, located right over officer's country. The wardroom, officer's galley, and all the staterooms except for the captain's. His cabin was located just aft of the bridge. During Officer's Call, the crew would line up by department or division; Deck, Engineering, Administration & Supply. Muster would be held and then the officers would file up from the wardroom to take reports and pass the word to the crew.

Access from the wardroom up to the main deck was through a large hatch. The hatches to below decks had to be large enough for heavy machinery to be removed and replaced.

This particular hatch was kept open permanently, except for General Quarters. To prevent water from coming in during heavy seas, or keep someone from falling through it, a small structure had been built to fit over the opening. We called it the Dog House. It was just tall enough for a small screen door facing aft on one end, and then tapered down to the deck on the other end.

As the officers came up the ladder from the wardroom, even the shorter ones had to duck a little. LT Wyman never, ever ducked enough and it was something the whole crew watched for each day. Up he'd come and BONK! He would hit his head. Sometimes he would even knock his hat off. On those days, he would have to go back down and retrieve it and if we were lucky, we would get a double header.

One day, the unbelievable happened. Mr. Wyman bent just right and didn't bump his head. He stepped through the little screen door and stood up and stretched out to his full 6' 8" and a huge smile spread from ear to ear. Just then someone from down below hollered his name. He spun around and went to stick his head in the door to see who was calling him. Smack! He nailed himself right in the forehead. The laughter was so loud, they had to re-call order in the ranks

We're not through with Mr. Wyman yet. As I said earlier, we were underway to Ponape and Mr. Wyman was OOD on the Bridge.

During most of our cruising in and around the Trust Territories, we were not on a tight schedule. Sometimes we put in a lot of steaming time between islands. These waters were rich with fishing floats, most of which had come off Japanese fishing nets.

Many of the crew members collected them. So, as a morale factor, the skipper passed the word to the OODs that if a nice float was spotted, at their discretion, they could slow down or turn around to pick it up. The key word here was discretion.

It was just about time for the noon meal. We were cruising in the open ocean. The sea swells were only running about two or three feet with an occasional larger wave coming along. The ship was heading into the sea which gave the *Basswood* a nice easy gait and all was well.

Some of the crew members were lined up in the vestibule forward of the mess deck waiting for chow. I was in sick bay typing a report. The cooks and mess cooks were scurrying around putting the last minute touches on the big mid-day meal. The baked potatoes were done and a mess cook was putting them into serving bowls and placing them on the mess deck tables. The other mess cook was setting out the condiments and bug juice (Kool-Aid). The two junior cooks were slicing the beef rib roasts and placing them on serving platters. The senior cook Bobby Green had five gallons of homemade vegetable beef soup bubbling on top of the stove. He had just shoved two large sheet cakes in the oven for dessert.

I felt the ship start to turn. When it had turned about 90 degrees, it took a heavy snap roll. I tipped into my typewriter as the chair slid out from under me. Water came in through my improvised air scoops and wet both me and my typing down. At the same time, there was this terrible commotion in the port passageway, and the worst screaming and cussing I'd ever heard.

I opened the sick bay door to find the decks in the port passageway awash with soup.

I peeked in the door of the galley and the oven was open. Bobby was cussing up a blue streak and loading his apron with Idaho Potatoes. His cakes were burnt as goo stuck to the sides of the oven. On the other side of the galley on the mess deck, the bug juice was everywhere and the mess deck was a fucking disaster. I thought to myself, *I guess he does cuss with the appropriate provocation.*

I followed Bobby and his potatoes out to the buoy deck. We watched him cuss out and throw potatoes at Mr. Wyman with an arm that would have done a big league baseball pitcher proud. The OOD was ducking this way and that, trying to keep from getting hit, while he apologized to the irate cook.

The OOD had missed seeing the rogue wave that was coming towards them, and turned right into the trough which caused the ship to take a violent roll.

When he ran out of ammo, Bobby returned to the galley and he and his cooks and mess cooks quietly cleaned up the mess. Needless to say, there was no soup or dessert with that day's noon meal. Nobody said shit to Bobby about his outburst. It was always something on the *Basswood*. In Ponape, it was going to be my turn to provide that something.

15 PONAPE ~ DOC TAKES IT IN THE KISSER

Ponape was a pretty island, like all of them were. When you got closer though, you could see the western influence. There was a small dock, just big enough for us to tie the ship up. Everything in and around the town was either made entirely of rusted corrugated tin or roofed with it. The local natives had once been able to build beautiful thatched houses that would stand up to all but the worst of the pacific storms. If it got blown down, they would harvest the materials from the jungle and build a new one. The art was being lost with the infringement of traders and missionaries. Now they lived in ugly, rusty tin shacks that were blown down almost every time there was a storm, requiring them to buy new materials from the traders.

We were going to be in port here for two nights. We would work local aids to navigation in the morning, remain here the next night, and then head back to Guam the following morning. We found the bar. It was typical, made partly of corrugated tin and partly with plywood. It had a few beat-up tables and chairs, a rough plank bar, and a concrete floor.

But hey, it had rum and beer and Guns and I were doing fine. We were buying some drinks for the locals and getting along well. I had bought the little native gal sitting next to me a couple cokes. We were communicating as best we could. That evening, she invited me outside and found us a nice grassy spot under a moonlit tropical sky. It was a lovely evening and you could see many of the constellations, including the Southern Cross. We did what came naturally, and then went back to the bar. It was another great night of liberty in paradise.

Let's talk about me a little bit. I was a single, twenty-seven year old hospital corpsman first class. I'm 5 foot 9 inches tall and at the time weighed about 180 pounds. I guess if I had to describe myself, I would say that I was a bit better than average looking. At least the girls thought so. While I was in the tropics, I had a good tan and my light brown hair was sun and seawater bleached to kind of a corn silk gold. Both the Micronesian and Asian girls were fascinated with my fair hair, both on my head and my arms.

When I was aboard the ship, I did my job and I was good at it. Ashore I was a walking erection, looking for somewhere to stick it. After I took care of that, I would turn to more cultivated pursuits like learning about the place and the people and their culture.

I readily admit that I did my fair share of drinking. I preferred rum and coke, but would drink whatever was available. I'm normally a happy go lucky guy. When I drink, I get to be an even happier guy. In other words, I'm not a mean or violent drunk. When I'm drunk, I love everybody. One thing though, my drinking did not prevent me from having bouts of pure stupidity. My second night of liberty in Ponape pretty much confirmed that.

I was standing back on the fantail that afternoon when I saw, what I considered to be, a fine specimen of what these Ponape islanders once were. He was a handsome man with a very muscular upper body. He was wearing a red loincloth and was paddling a fifteen-foot outrigger canoe in from one of the outer islands. Little did I know that I would meet him later in the day.

That evening, we were back at the bar drinking and having a good time. There was no sign of my little gal. I figured she would probably be in later. First we all told a round of sea stories. Then, as we had a few more drinks, things deteriorated into strength games. Why men do this while they're drunk and at their weakest and least coordinated, I'll never know. It just is. Well, there was arm wrestling and other contests going on and the natives were becoming interested and wanted to join in.

This is where my judgment failed me. With my Judo classes back in Hawaii, I figured I could show these guys a thing or two. When I asked for a volunteer, the guy I had seen in the canoe that afternoon stepped up. He was about twenty and I was sure, just as strong as he looked. Micronesian island men are not very tall as a rule, but they are really built, just what you'd expect from guys who spend their days working hard to carve a life out of their environment. I was going to show him something called a *tominagi*. It's a Judo sacrifice move where your opponent rushes you, then you grab his forearms and go to the ground. At the same time, you plant one foot on the floor and put the other one in his mid-section with your leg flexed. The way it works is that you use his forward momentum and as you are pulling his arms towards and past your body, you straighten out your leg and propel him over your head.

In sport Judo, you maintain your hold on your opponent's arms and guide him to the floor or mat. Instead, I let go and he slammed, upside down, into the wall a few feet behind us.

I got up, turned back to the bar laughing with the guys, and took a sip of my drink. The next thing I knew, I was in the air at the top of my opponents extended arms, and then I was flying towards the deck face first at about forty knots. I did not have time to break my fall and landed on my forehead, nose, and upper jaw. My nose broke and one of my upper front teeth went skittering across the concrete floor. My other front teeth were just hanging by a thread of tissue. My upper lip was cut and I figured my upper jaw may have been fractured.

The native kid was really sorry and he didn't know what to do, although someone said they saw him pick up my tooth and swallow it. He fussed and fussed around me and I told him it was okay, it was my fault. Then, a couple of my guys escorted me back to the ship. I was sitting on the mess deck trying to tolerate a lukewarm cup of coffee. I had already looked in the mirror. My mom would not have recognized me.

One of the crewmen on the mess deck said, "What are you going to do, Doc?"

My slurred response was, "Since the nearest medical facility is in Guam about four days away, I guess I will have to fix myself." *Boy that was not going to be fun at all*, I thought.

In sick bay, I gently rinsed my mouth with some sterile saline solution, and then worked my remaining front teeth back where they belonged. The next step was a son-of-a-bitch. I looked through my instruments for something to straighten my nose. I have the most sensitive nose in the world. If you just flick it with a fingertip, it brings tears to my eyes.

I found a couple dental instruments with round handles that would fit up my nostrils. I wrapped two of them with gauze and fit one up each nostril while I stood in front of a mirror. Then, I squeezed them together like pliers and moved the bones and cartilage in my nose until it was back where it was supposed to be. At least externally. I still have a badly deviated septum. When I stopped crying, I splinted my nose in place. I used hard cotton dowels and taped them to each side of my nose with a big strip of adhesive tape to hold everything in place until it healed. And last, I used a couple of folded triangular bandages (slings) to tie my jaw closed, just in case it was broken.

On the way back to Guam, I ate clear soups with a piece of surgical tubing poked through the hole where my tooth was missing. When we got back, we were only going to be there three days before we were off again. I was really hoping that by the time we got to Guam, everything would be healing well and there were no complications to prevent me from sailing on our next trip.

Upon arriving on Guam, I reported to the Navy Base Dental Clinic. Since we were leaving so soon, the dentist said he would fix the missing tooth with a temporary flipper plate. He would do a more permanent job on it when we got back. He said the front teeth that I had put back in place, may or may not take, and I should eat soft food and be careful how I bite down on them until they tighten up. My upper jaw did have a hairline fracture, but there was nothing to do for it but let it heal. All and all, I felt that my stupidity had resulted in the best possible outcome. Now, if I'd only learned something from the experience.

I did, however, get a lot of teasing from the crew. "Fucking Doc gets a couple of drinks in him and tries to take on the toughest guy in the joint." Oh well, just one more story added to my legend. On our next stop, it would be the ships turn to add to its legend and help earn it the reputation of being an "Animal Farm."

But first, let me tell you another fish story. One of our many colorful characters aboard was a radioman. For the purpose of this story, we'll call him Winters. Winters was good enough at his job and had recently been promoted to RM2, a second class petty officer. Most of the time, Petty Officer Winters was a pretty funny guy, but he had little use for military discipline and frequently could be heard bitching about it.

I didn't really understand his attitude. The Coast Guard could be as disciplined as any of the military services when discipline was called for. But being in a small service and in particular on a small ship, life tended to be pretty laid back. Winters had a problem with any authority at all.

I don't know if RM2 Winters was one of our onboard tokers, but with his general attitude, he could have been. His crowning achievement took place late one night while we were tied up in the Trust Territories. Winters had returned from liberty drunk or high or both. He noticed one of the crew members was fishing off the fantail and had just landed about a sixty-pound Pacific Tuna, an *ulua*. Winters asked him what he was going to do with it and the guy said he was just going to throw it back. Petty Officer Winters asked if he could have it.

He took the fish, and for some reason thought it would be hilarious to sneak into the officer's wardroom and place the still very much alive fish on their dining table.

That's exactly what he did. The fish flopped around getting scales and fish slime all over the table before falling to the deck and flopping around some more there. This commotion woke one of the officers who saw Petty Officer Winters as he was sneaking out the door.

Winters was apprehended and put on report. He was scheduled for a Captain's Mast later in the week. A Captain's Mast is a form of non-judicial trial where commanding officers of ships can hand down punishment to members of their crew for less serious offences. A captain can award a monetary fine, a demotion in rank, or three days in the brig on bread and water. The brig can be any lockable compartment on the ship suitable for the purpose.

Well, old Winters' figured he was going to lose a stripe at the very least. So he prepared what he thought would, in his own fucked up mind, be a funny stunt. He cut one of his chevrons' off and then lightly re-attached it with some sort of adhesive.

The captain did, in fact, tell him, "Petty Officer Winters, you are hereby being reduced one rank for your childish stunt in the wardroom." Hearing this, now RM3 Winters raised his left arm and blew the stripe off. As it fluttered to the deck, the skipper said with a straight face," that was very amusing Seaman Winters, now blow the other one off."

So, the dumb shit lost two stripes for a stupid prank. Well, it takes all kinds. The CO let Seaman Winters stew in his own juice for a month and then had a heart-to-heart with him and decided to give him his rank back. The episode ended up costing RM2 Winters a month of severely reduced pay and less than perfect conduct marks for that marking period. We all thought that was pretty big of the skipper to do that.

16 PALAU AND THE BATTLE OF THE BOOM-BOOM ROOM

This was going to be a long trip. And before we even got started, there were immunizations to be given for the Vietnam segment of the trip. Cholera, plague, gamma globulin, and malaria prophylaxis were to be started eight weeks before we arrived in country. The guys always groused about shots, but when they saw me giving myself my own shots, they shut up.

We were making three stops in the Palau Islands; Babeldaob, Angaur, and Koror. After leaving Palau we would be sailing directly to Southeast Asia. The trust territory islands that we had visited were an interesting novelty and we would enjoy Palau, but the Asia trip is what we were all waiting for. Vietnam aside, there were some great liberty ports in our future.

We tied up the ship at Babeldaob Island, the largest and most westernized of the Palau Group. We spent a few days there and I got lucky again. Our next stop was Angaur where there was, you guessed it, a Coast Guard LORAN Station.

The station was built on an old Japanese air strip from WWII and there were a couple Zero fighter planes rotting in the jungle off one side of the air strip. If you looked out to the southwest, some seven miles away, you could just barely make out Peleliu Island where one of the bloodiest battles in the Pacific took place. One thousand eight hundred Americans and 10,700 Japanese died there.

The Palau Islands were beautiful as islands go, but the long association with westerners on the larger islands had changed the locals. Some had lost the friendly, childlike persona that you found on the more isolated islands. Our first hint of that was on Angaur. A seaman named Vincent was out drinking with some of the local natives. They were riding around in a beat-up old Toyota pickup. Vincent was in the back with three or four of the locals. He was pretty shitfaced and must have said or done something wrong. They threw him out of the truck while it was running at about thirty miles an hour. Some of our other crewmembers found him stumbling along the road, brought him to the ship, and then went and found me.

That old cliché that God takes care of little babies and drunks must be true because Vincent had nothing broken. All he was wearing at the time were cut offs. He did, however, have almost a total body abrasion and the wounds were full of coral (crushed coral is what the island roads were made of) and I had to get that out. I used a small surgical scrub brush and pHisoHex soap to scrub the coral out of his wounds. Then, I painted him with an antiseptic tincture and wrapped him in sterile gauze. The poor bastard looked like a mummy and was miserable for the next couple of weeks while he healed. He was a walking scab.

Our next stop was Koror. As it turned out, some of the local guys had a definite animosity towards outsiders, particularly a ship full of horny sailors.

We arrived early and went right to work servicing the buoys and other aids to navigation around the island. Then we tied up and liberty was granted. Most of us settled in at a bar we found near the waterfront. The crewmembers were mesmerized by a local gal who could open the top of a steel beer can with her teeth. She just sunk her front teeth in the top of the can and gnawed the lid off of it just like a John Wayne can opener.

Yours truly scored with another Palauan girl who was drinking in the bar and I went off with her to close the deal, so I missed the excitement. When we returned a couple of hours later, the bar was deserted and the bartender said that everyone had gone over to the Boom-Boom Room. The Boom-Boom Room was as close as there was to a night club on the island. It had a juke box and a dance floor and served San Miguel Beer from the Philippines, and mixed drinks.

My new best friend and I decided to have a couple of drinks at the bar and then head over to the Boom-Boom Room, located a couple of miles from where we were currently drinking. By the time we got there, it was pretty much over with. I arrived just in time to patch up one of my crewmen who, according to him, was minding his own business when he got hit in the face by a rock the size of a bowling ball. He was a mess with a bad laceration and some loose teeth, but nothing that I couldn't handle.

The Boom-Boom Room was in a large native-style building built on stilts about four feet off the ground with stairs going up to a front porch. Inside there were a number of tables and chairs, a bar, and a good-sized dance floor. The place had windows all around that were just open holes that could be closed with thatched shutters in a storm. These were all open.

The ship's crew had been having a great time drinking and dancing. Most of the available women on the island were there with them. As you might imagine, this pissed off the male population of Koror and they had planned a well-coordinated attack. They had cached a large supply of rocks outside under the windows. Then they

63

surrounded the place and started the war. These guys could really throw rocks, shit, they could knock birds out of the tops of palm trees.

Our guys were catching hell. They were trapped and had nothing to throw back until one of the crew discovered the hard liquor storage, row after row of booze in bottles. There must have been a two or three year supply stocked there. To the bartenders continued screams of NO!, our guys started throwing the only thing they had, full bottles of booze. Then, one of our bigger guys figured the juke box would make a good weapon. He tipped it out one of the windows where a group of natives had gathered. After a bit, our side pretty much regrouped and had the enemy in retreat. I had just arrived and the crew used the lull in the battle to get back to the ship.

The bar proprietor arrived just before we got underway the next morning. The Island's Administrator had a bill for $18,000.00. The captain said he would submit the bill to Coast Guard COMMARSEC in Guam and that it would probably have to go to the Coast Guard 14th District Office in Honolulu for settlement. The Island Administrator then informed us that the *Basswood* and her crew were persona non grata on the Island of Koror and that we would not be allowed ashore when we next returned to work in the area. As we sailed away licking our wounds, our thoughts would soon turn to the next stop on our fantastic voyage.

Palau had not been all bedding babes and bar room brawls. They were beautiful islands and I had managed to see quite a lot while I was there. The young ladies and others I had befriended shared much about their culture and islands with me. I was often taken to the best places to see as well as some wonderful diving spots. Nearly all of them had access to a boat. I really had to wonder at the diversity of sea life and the clarity of the water. They showed me isolated beaches and hidden lagoons that were teeming with many kinds of fish. You could see the bottom sixty or eighty feet below. It was like God's own aquarium and I had to wonder if all the oceans were like this before modern man polluted them.

Our next stop was the Philippines. Guns had told me so much about the place we were going, it just made me want to see it all the more. There wasn't anything cultural about it. The town of Olongapo was a boom town which had grown up over the years outside the big Subic Bay Naval Base. The sole purpose of this town was to fill the base needs of the American service man. These were specifically, eating, drinking and screwing, not necessarily in that order.

"Yeah Doc, you're going to love those little Filipina girls and wait until you see Olongapo right outside the main gate of Subic Bay Naval

Base. As far as you can see straight down the road, miles of hooker bars, restaurants, street vendors and short time hotels."

"Sounds like Sailor Heaven," I said.

"It is, you just wait and see. It's just the first of a bunch of great liberty ports we're gonna be visiting. You won't ever want to go back to the States."

"Shut up Guns, I'm getting a stiff dick."

We sailed on for a few more days, as I waited in anticipation of my first visit to the country they called the Pearl of the Orient.

17 THE PHILIPPINES, MY FIRST TIME

The Philippine archipelago consists of 7,107 islands and is about 1,150 miles long. We entered the archipelago from the east at about mid-point by sailing through the San Bernardino Straits between the southern tip of Luzon and North Samar. We then sailed north threading our way between Ticao and Masbate Islands and further north on the Sibuan Sea. We then went west through the Verde Dip Passe and north again up the west coast of Luzon past the entrance to Manila Bay and Bataan and on to Subic Bay.

It was a beautiful trip as we steamed overnight and for most of two days. Since the Philippines are volcanic islands with many active volcanoes on the night portion of our trip, we were treated to the sight of red glowing mountaintops along the way. During the first day, we came upon a huge pod of small whales traveling in the same direction. They were all around the ship as far as the eye could see.

As we got closer to Manila Bay, the surrounding waters were crowded with all kinds of watercraft from large powered outriggers called pump boats, to small comfits carrying local trade goods, as well as ferries and the largest oceangoing freighters. Manila Bay has been an important sea port since the early Spanish times, when it was a stopover on the China Silk Route.

When we pulled into Subic Bay and the U.S. Navy Base located there, we saw another very busy port. It was the middle of the Vietnam War. As Vietnam was only about 500 miles to the west, this was a very busy place. Naval ships of all kinds were tied up to the docks or anchored out. Supply tenders and liberty boats were zipping back and forth across the harbor. Since this was also a ship repair facility, as well as a supply depot, the base was spread out all over the place and there were many large building as well as dry docks.

The crew was fever pitched with anticipation. The rumors about Olongapo just outside the main gate had been all anyone had talked about for days. And now here we were. For most of us, we were mere moments away from getting our first look at this notorious sailor paradise.

Liberty was going to turn out to be an interesting exercise. According to Navy rules, only officers could wear civvies and everyone had Cinderella liberty (return by midnight).

Our CO said, "Screw that, we're in the Coast Guard, not the Navy or Marines. My guys are wearing civvies if they feel like it and liberty for them will last until 0800 in the morning or longer if they have a 48 or 72 hour pass."

We had fun with it. We were tied up outboard to a Navy Destroyer at least twice as big as our ship. Our first liberty party went ashore, about twenty guys, all in civilian clothes.

The Navy quarterdeck watch saluted everyone in the liberty party and addressed them all as Sir. They must have wondered that there were so many officers aboard such a small ship.

Coming back from liberty in the mornings, we had to deal with the Marine gate guards putting us on report for being AWOL because nobody was supposed to stay out overnight. We would bring the booking sheets to our XO, and he would tear them up. Sometimes we would be showered, shaved and heading back out the gate again while the same Marine was on duty. Pretty soon, they just started shaking their heads and muttering, "Fucking Coast Guard."

That first day Guns Gunderson gave me the chef's tour of Olongapo. As you go out the gate, the first thing that assails you is the smell. There is a bridge right outside the front gate that crosses over a sewer masquerading as a river. I think you could almost walk across it without a bridge.

Down in this river under the bridge are young kids and teenagers in canoes begging for coins. They would have nets on poles to catch the coins. Some of the more sadistic squids liked to throw the coins out of their reach so they would have to dive into that nasty river after them. Yeah, there are people like that. I call them assholes.

After the bridge is Magsaysay Drive. It's straight as an arrow for about five miles. Every inch of this street is filled with street vendors, kids who shine shoes, pick pockets, street walkers, night clubs and hooker bars, restaurants, and short time hotels. Now, the smell was more like sour beer, vomit, sex, and pork cooking on outside grills. It was wonderful and the sound was raucous with vendors hawking their wares, jeepney horns and loud American rock music coming out of all the club doors. It was pure aphrodisiac for sailors.

Guns had already schooled me in some points of survival in Olongapo. It was all pretty common sense stuff. Don't carry a wallet. If you carry a wallet in your back pocket, someone will cut it off you with a very sharp knife, and probably take part of your ass with it. Just bring your I.D. card and however much cash you want to spend. The I.D. goes in one front pocket and the cash in the other one. Don't put cigarettes or change in your shirt pockets. Some kid will run up to you, slap the bottom of your pocket, then snatch whatever was in it out of the air and run. Change also goes in your front pants pockets. Cigarettes go in your socks.

Be nice to the shoe shine kids, especially if you come out in dress whites. Let them shine your shoes or give them a little tip. If you piss them off, they will come up behind you and put black polish on your white uniform. Don't take a jeepney and if you do, don't go alone or you may find yourself off on a side street and rolled.

A jeepney is the main form of local public transportation in the Philippines. They were originally made from WWII jeeps. The backs were extended and covered with a roof and a couple parallel benches were installed for passengers. Every Jeepney has its own gaudy paint job, inside and out, with lots of religious motifs. They have lots of chrome horns and/or horses bolted to the hoods. A jeepney will carry as many people as can be squeezed into it. Don't give the driver a large bill, unless you have a collection of Japanese Occupation Pesos you want to add to. That's what he will give you for change. They're not legal tender, so you can't spend them.

He told me to remember everything off the main street is off limits. That's why they have an MP or Shore Patrol on almost every corner.

With us having overnight liberty, he said we would be able to get away with it, but don't go there or off into the neighborhood until you've met a gal you like and trust. In that case, the girl will take care of you. So I was good to go.

"Okay Doc, the mission for today is RECON and to get you laid, of course. We'll take a tour up and down the street, check out a few clubs, get our ashes hauled, and then try and find a place we feel comfortable hanging out in and make it our place. We have a lot of stuff going for us. We have overnight liberty and can wear civvies and we will be spending quite a bit of time here. If we find a regular place and get a 'semi-steady girl' who works there, life will be good for us here."

"What do you mean, semi-steady girls?"

"Well, one of the things these girls will say to you right away is 'you no butterfly Joe' which means stick with one girl and not go flitting around from girl to girl. You'll find that even these little bar girls would rather have a steady guy. And if they think you're their steady, they will take good care of you."

Guns saw a place he liked and said, "Let's try here."

We walked up a flight of stairs. A couple of very cute young ladies detached themselves from the bar and came up to us.

"Hi Joe, you looking for girl?"

68

Guns told them, "This is his first time in the P.I., you take good care of him."

One of them looked at me and said, "Okay Joe. You come with Luz. I love you long time."

Everybody from the States was Joe (G.I. Joe) until they get to know your name. It's left over from the Second World War. Guns and I each paired off and our girls led us off to their rooms.

This was the first time I ever paid anyone to have sex, so it was a really new experience for me. I was nervous. They try to make it really easy for you, so, when you and the girl are together in the room, you only have to worry about one thing. The transaction takes place at the bar just like paying for a drink. They call it a bar fine. What it amounts to is that she has to pay for the time she is not at the bar working and hustling drinks. It was 55 pesos, about $12.00. She got her cut from this, plus whatever she could negotiate with her horny customer.

When we got to the room, I explained to her about it being my first time and I might have trouble getting it up.

She said, "No worry Joe, I fix."

And she did.

When we got done, Guns and his girl were waiting for us with drinks. His girl said, "Oh my, you take long time, Joe."

My girl said, "Joe is good lover. He love me long time," as she smiled and caressed the hair on my arm.

These girls will do whatever they can to stroke your ego. To make you look good in front of your buddies. Guns and I bid our girls adieu, or *paalam* as it would be in Tagalog. We continued our search for a place to hang out, which included us getting laid at least once more.

"See Doc, I told you these little Filipina girls really know how to take care of man."

"Yeah Guns, I think I'm getting the drift."

One of the things I witnessed as we wandered around Olongapo were the young girls who would stick their heads out of a filthy alley to whisper, "Joe, I give you blow job, one peso."

Most were not good looking or had a physical deformity, while others would have a naked baby riding on one hip. It was pretty damned sad when the sex trade was all there was and you were an outcast in that business. I usually tossed them something. I could not do otherwise. I guess if I was going to hang around in the third world, I would have to get used to this and develop a little harder shell.

Later that afternoon, we finally found a place that just felt right. It was the Coconut Grove Night Club and it was not too far from the front gate, maybe three or four blocks. It was a big place with live music and theme nights. One night the girls might be in cowboy outfits. The next they would dress like cheeleaders. The band could play Country-Western as well as anything that was on the American Top Forty Charts. And most of the time, they played it as well as the original artists.

The bars in Olongapo specialized in knowing what young Americans wanted and went out of their way to provide it. And what was that? It was a cold beer in your hand a hot girl on your knee and loud rock or Country-Western music, depending on what part of the States you came from. The Coconut Grove did an exceptional job at this. And this was where I met Mari Sol Salceda, who would become my steady girl when we were in Olongapo.

Mari Sol was a nice gal.

She was a few years older than me, and she spoke better English than most of the other girls.

She didn't look her age, but told me that she had a sixteen-year-old daughter. She was spending part of the money she earned to send her to a private Catholic School. Mari Sol did not seem like a prostitute to me, but rather just someone getting by the best way she could.

When I was in town, she would not go out with anyone else. Basically, we would dance some and then she would go off and hustle the squids for drinks until they had to go home. Then she would get off and we would spend the night together. There was never a bar fine that way and I could use the money for other forms of entertainment for her and me.

During some weekend days, we would go on outings with some of the other guys and their girls to a resort town called White Rock Beach. There were beach cabanas and it also had a big swimming pool with an island in the middle and a bandstand at one end. There were restaurants and food stands and a duck pin bowling alley. The poor old Navy and Marine Corps guys never got to see any of this stuff. I was really glad that I was in the Coast Guard.

Well, girls were not the only thing we came to Subic Bay for. While we were taking turns on liberty, the duty sections were taking on additional food supplies, fuel, potable water, and ordnance. We received two additional .50 caliber machine guns, more ammo, a case of M-16s with cases of both loaded magazines in bandoleers and boxed ammo as well as a couple of cases of half-pound granular TNT swimmer grenades. Guns had also ordered a ground mount for a fifty just in case he had to take one ashore and some BDUs (fatigues) in a variety of sizes.

Liberty is over, boys and girls. It's time to see what Vietnam holds in store for us.

18 INTO THE BREACH, NOT QUITE

Our first month of duty in the war zone was not too exciting, except for the fact that we were there. The first stop on the way to Vietnam was Sattahip, Thailand to the Army Supply Depot located nearby. We were going to pick up some portable freezers and refrigerators full of supplies for our LORAN Station on Con Son Island in Vietnam. Sattahip was in Southern Thailand, not far from the Royal Thai Air Base in Udorn where the U.S. Air Force had a major presence during the Vietnam War.

One of the things the CO wanted to get done while we were in Thailand was to fill sandbags to place around our four machine gun mounts. He told our new Chief Bosun John Paneria to appoint some volunteers, borrow a truck from the supply depot, and make it happen. You should have heard the bitching and moaning, but then when the work detail returned later that day, they were all smiles.

As it turns out, some of the local bar girls were at the beach on some kind of a busman's holiday. Most of the guys in the detail had gotten laid or at least set up for liberty later that evening. Who the fuck said 'never volunteer'?

After we were loaded and the gun mounts were finished, we set sail for Con Son.

We would be going back to Sattahip once more in order to return the 'fridge boxes to the Army Depot. All the LORAN stations in the Vietnam theater of operations, including the one on Con Son, were the newer Class C stations. They were longer range and much more accurate than the old Loran-A stations. Loran-C stations had a crew of twenty-nine men.

Con Son was notable for one thing, the infamous Tiger Cage Prison. It had been used by the Vietnamese for years to hold political prisoners. The cells had no windows or doors and only steel bars for a roof. There was nothing for the prisoners to see but the sky above and there was no protection from the elements. We were all really glad to get out of that depressing place.

Our return trip to Sattahip was just a quick turn around and then off to Phu Quoc. Phu Quoc is the largest island in Vietnam. It is located in the Gulf of Thailand just 7 ½ miles from Cambodia. Phu Quoc was also known for making the best Nuoc Mam Sauce in Vietnam (fermented fish sauce). The Vietnamese eat it on everything and you could smell it for miles if the wind was right.

Our work there was going to be near An Thoi, where the Southern Naval Support Activities were located.

This was also the home of U.S. Coast Guard Squadron One Division 11 and also a Navy Swift Boat Base. They all lived and tied up together on a floating island of barges including a couple of 'APLs' for crew sleeping and eating, repair facilities, and a floating dock. This conglomeration of floating buildings had been using its own anchors to hold them in place. This was really not satisfactory with the weather, winds, currents, and tides.

We were going to install mooring buoys for them so they would stay put under almost any conditions. This was going to be a demonstration of deck seamanship for the textbooks. I watched in awe while our deck force performed this miracle working with some of the biggest, heaviest and most dangerous ground tackle in existence.

The buoys themselves were very large. Lying on their sides, they stood twice as high as a six and a half foot man or about thirteen feet across. Each buoy was to have three legs of large chain. The steel rings that held these chains together at the bottom of the buoy weighed more than 100 pounds. At the bottom of each leg was an anchor of a size that was once used on Navy cruisers. It was going to take a large crane located on the beach as well as the deck of our ship, a large barge alongside, and our own boom to do the job.

When it was all laid out perfectly, they would cut it loose one leg at a time. It would just be a blur, like one of the those domino tricks they do on TV. God help you if you were in the path of any of this gear. You would be lucky if they could find all the pieces of you. We had been hampered with some bad weather. It took us thirteen days to complete the work. But the job had been done right and no one had been injured.

During what little down time we had in An Thoi, there wasn't much to do. There was a dirt runway carved out of the jungle of the U Minh Forest and there was a Congressman Mendel Rivers beer drinking club. It was like a firebase with a beer locker. It was surrounded by sand bags and barbed wire, and it had cold beer and a juke box. Congressman Rivers had many such places built for the troops throughout the country. They were all the same, prefabricated with a big sign on top of the roof with the Congressman's name.

Between running time and our stops in Thailand and Con Son as well as the thirteen days in An Thoi, we had been out of the Philippines better than a month.

The skipper made a happy crew when he informed us at quarters that we would be returning to the Philippines. Coconut Grove, here we come.

19 THE OLONGAPO FLU

During our trip back to Subic Bay, we picked up a big storm cell north of Luzon. We were heading south and so was the storm front. We had a typhoon in front of us, one behind us, and another off to the west of our position.   You don't outrun storms in a buoy tender, so the skipper started looking for a place to hide. The closest place he found where we might be protected from the storm was a point of land on Luzon, north of Subic Bay. It was Naulo Point. The point curved around a small protected bay with a good anchorage. There was also a Coast Guard LORAN Station there.

We pulled into the little bay and put down anchors both fore and aft to keep the ship in place should there be a heavy blow. We stayed a couple of days while the storms passed. While we there, we had a chance to visit with the LORAN crew. It was a nice place if you had to be on isolated duty. Some of the guys had built native houses outside the base where they lived with their Filipina girlfriends. A small community had also built up near the station.

This was something I kept stored it in the back of my mind for future reference, should I ever find myself assigned to a LORAN Station.

We pulled up our anchors and once again set out for Subic Bay and Olongapo, which was only a couple of days away. This time we tied up right at the dock, but as we came through the bay, we saw that a carrier battle group was in port. This could not be good. We're talking seven or eight thousand additional swabbies and jarheads to contend with.

I guess we would now see if the rumors were true about the Navy having 5,000 card-carrying hookers in Olongapo who came in to the Navy Base for VD checks each week. Well, it sounded like something the Navy would do, but who knows? The first indication we had that this may be true was that the Marine Gate Guards had counters. If you were number five thousand and one, you did not get to pass through the gate until somebody returned. That's when we really became thankful for overnight liberty. We usually had more than one night off, and when we got out, we could stay out. The carrier was not as big a problem as we thought it would be. It seemed that a large percentage of these carrier sailors never left the ship, or if they did, they stayed on the base. Go figure, squids!

Well, as it turns out, fate was not through fucking with us yet. This monster crowd of human sea life had brought a new strain of Asian flu into port. My guys started to get sick. There was no vaccine in the system to treat this strain of flu. All I could do was treat the symptoms. As a result of this little epidemic, we spent eighteen days in Subic Bay instead of three or four, which was both good and bad. It was bad because almost eighty percent of my crew was sick. Good because I spent almost every night in Olongapo.

I would hold sick call twice a day and check for new cases. I made rounds to follow up on my guys who were down with the disease and make sure they had APCs and access to enough fluids. I had the cooks forcing fluids at meal time and serving lots of chicken broth and other clear soups. We just let it run its course. I didn't get sick, so I spent my free nights with Mari Sol.

One other bad thing was that these extra days in port messed up our work schedule. We would be rushing around from place to place playing catch up. It would no longer be such a leisurely patrol. After the fact, it would all kind of seem like a blur of different countries and islands. We were going back to Guam next to pick up some buoys for Okinawa and then we would be there for two days, back to the Philippines, and then back to Vietnam for a few months.

Shit, we endured day after day at sea and some really terrible weather on the way back to Guam. We had not planned on staying long, but we arrived just behind a typhoon that had torn up Saipan pretty bad. We got tagged to help in the relief effort. The storm had contaminated their aviation fuel and they needed both jet fuel and high octane aviation gas for their search planes and helicopters. There was a tanker on the way, but we could get their quicker with emergency supplies. They loaded ninety-two fifty-five gallon drums on the *Basswood*'s buoy deck and lashed them down.

It was late when we left on one of the worst nights at sea I had ever experienced. The typhoon was gone, but in its wake it had left some really horrible sea conditions. It was about 130 miles to Saipan. I thought the ship was going to start doing cartwheels before we got there. We were taking water over the bridge wings and sometimes over the flying bridge which is more than forty feet above the water line of our ship, or if you prefer, above sea level.

Then, in the middle of the night, the emergency claxon went off. Some of those drums had broken loose and were flying around the buoy deck. The damage control crews were standing by above both sides of the buoy deck with charged fire hoses. The deck force down below worked to wrestle the 500-pound drums back in place and get them secured. Everybody else was prepared to abandon ship if the worst happened. One stray spark in the wrong place and I might not be here writing this.

We made it in okay and got our cargo delivered. I patched up some injured guys from the deck force; cuts, scrapes, sprains, nothing really serious, thank God. One of those drums could have crushed a man. We rested in port for several hours until the weather let up. Everyone was able to get a little sack time. Then, we headed back to Guam. We took care of our business there and headed out again.

By November 9th we were in Okinawa. Okinawa was another interesting place. It was the largest of the Ryuku Islands. It was also another bloody campaign of WWII. Right next door on Ishima Island was where famous WWII war correspondent Ernie Pyle was killed. Okinawa was part of the Japanese Empire, but it had been a U.S. Protectorate since the end of WWII.

The U.S. military had a large presence on the island and it was a strategic location with the large Kadena Air Force Base located just outside of Naha and both Army and Marine bases on the north side of the island. The place Guns and I were interested in was Namenoue, specifically, the red-light district. If you're a movie buff, this was also the home of the Teahouse of the August Moon, where the movie of the same name was shot starring a very young Marlon Brando. We were not, however, movie buffs. We were pussy buffs.

We found Namenoue and in short order, we were sharing a drink with a pair of beautiful, porcelain-skinned, Japanese girls. Prostitution was illegal in Okinawa, but someone forgot to tell the girls. We were in civvies this day, and for some reason, the girl I was with thought I was a B-52 pilot. It was not in my heart to disappoint her. So, off we went into the wild blue yonder.

We had a good chance to look around and this place was like a miniature Tokyo, crowded, some tall buildings, and lots of neon. We also visited Kadena AFB and their NCO Club. The club had a slot room bigger than some you would find in Las Vegas.

The next day we were going to be working on the north side of the island, so we would be anchoring there for the night. The north shore also had a White Rock Beach and villages one, two, and three. We dropped the hook and a group of us decided to go ashore to have a drink. We took one of the small boats and beached it on the Marine Base. We were in civvies and were a mixed bunch, with everything from a seaman apprentice to a chief warrant officer.

When we landed, we were immediately surrounded by a bunch of Okinawan Guards with 12-gauge riot guns. None of them spoke English. Finally, a Marine corporal showed up, checked our IDs and sorted things

75

out. He told us we were lucky we had not landed fifty yards to our right. It was some kind of army security base and it was guarded by big, mean dogs.

We were not able to get a drink at any of the clubs on base and stay together because of our mixed ranks. The Marines are fussy about that kind of stuff. We decided to go to the village just outside the gate. We spent the rest of the evening drinking beer at a skivvy house.

We passed the time talking with the mama-san and some of her girls taking a break from screwing Marines. Once again, I thanked my lucky stars that I was in the Coast Guard.

The jarheads were lined up out the door, probably in squad formation. There were four girls working the line. They were on cots about two feet apart. Each cot had a basin of water next to it. The girls would lay there with their legs apart and knees in the air. A marine would walk up, un-zip, climb on, and hump up and down until he got his rocks off. Then, he would climb off and the next guy in line would climb aboard.

About every third or fourth guy, the girls would squat over their basins and wash themselves out. It went on like that until we got tired of watching and went back to the ship. It's a good thing we were getting underway the next day, because after witnessing the Green Machine getting laid, I didn't think I would want to have sex for awhile.

I could not help thinking at the time, *in a week or so, these poor bastards will probably be in some leech-infested rice paddy getting shot at. Semper Fi, guys.*

As it turned out, Okinawa was not one of our favorite liberty ports. The girls were cold and all business, no fun at all. The rest of the place was pretty much of a rip-off, as well. Our next and last trip to Okinawa would just reinforce our general dislike for the place.

We shoved off the morning of the 14th. Our next stop would be Subic on the 19th to get briefed on our mission in Vietnam. At the same time, we would pick up the first two of the four Navy SEALS, who would be operating with us. They would also be putting much of the gear aboard that might be needed for operations from the ship.

We would pick up two more SEALS in Cat Lo near Vung Tau and receive the rest of their gear as well as our in country briefing before moving into the bays and rivers.

This would also be our last trip to Subic Bay and Olongapo. The crew was pretty broken up about that. Well, that's a sailor's life, and there would be new ports to explore before our odyssey was over.

20 OLONGAPO OUR LAST TIME ~ LUCKY RUNS AMOK

When we arrived in Subic Bay, the skipper, the XO, the navigation officer, and the ship's First Lieutenant CWO 3 Souza all attended a briefing with a couple of Navy four stripers and a Coast Guard Lieutenant Commander named Knapp. These guys were all from JSMACV or just MACV (Joint Services Military Advisory Command Vietnam). Also present were the first two SEALS, a Navy Lieutenant named Powers, and a second class petty officer, a radioman, that like all radiomen, was called Sparky. The *honchos* over in MACV had put their heads together and had been studying what our buoy tenders were doing and where they were working. That would be bays and rivers all over the country.

Navy SEALS were assigned aboard our ships to check for enemy activity, mines, and booby traps before we went ashore to do our A to N work. They had watched the Planetree while she was in country, then the *Basswood*, and then the ship that had relieved us after our first little excursion into Vietnam.

They decided that we were pretty innocuous as military units went, i.e., nobody paid much attention to us. In addition, we went into areas that they were interested in.

They came to the decision that they could get a better bang for their buck with the four-man SEAL team attached to our ships if they could use the ship as a base for some of their own operations. When we were in or near an area of interest, the team could be deployed on an operational hunter killer, harassment, or recon mission, whatever their command or the situation called for.

It was decided to go ahead with it and they put the additional gear aboard that they would need to run their operations as well as a 13-foot Boston Whaler like the skipper's gig. But it was a little different; it was painted black, had a mount for an M-60 machine gun, and had a much faster engine than the skipper's boat. It also had a Vietnamese one-cylinder outboard like all the local fishing boats used. They would use the unique sound of the fishing boat engine to sneak up on their targets.

It was agreed that when they left on an operation, it would be under cover of darkness. They would keep radio communications with the ship whenever possible and set up some crypto voice codes and identification signals to use for this purpose.

Our skipper asked, "What happens if we get in some heavy shit? We don't have a lot of fire power with only four .50 caliber machine guns."

He was told that both the ship and the SEALS would have direct radio access to units that could provide help in short order, like Navy PBRs (Patrol Boats, River) and Cobra Helicopter Gun Ships in the area.

Everybody agreed that it was a workable plan. We would pick up the other two SEALS in Cat Lo when we arrived in Vietnam. Then our CO would sit down with the local SEAL command to examine our schedule and see how it matched up with the SEAL commander's areas of interest. Using this information, they would set up a series of potential operations for the SEALS deploying from our ship.

The business was over. The SEALS gear was loaded aboard and it was time for us to deploy on a liberty patrol in Olongapo. However, before I explain that, I have to introduce you to Lucky. It doesn't matter what his real name was. To the crew of the *Basswood*, he would forevermore, just be known as Lucky.

Lucky came aboard when we arrived in Guam. He was a second class engineman and he looked like a real sailor. Lucky was not real big, about 5 foot 8 inches, but very muscular. He came by that build honestly. He was a gymnast in high school and later became very interested in that brand new (in our country) martial art called Karate. Most of us still thought Judo was hot stuff.

Lucky was dressed in a tailor-made uniform with his tie synched up tight and wings in his white hat. When he rolled up his sleeves, he also had the requisite tattoos on his forearms. As it turned out, he was a genuinely nice guy. They say he did a great job in the engine room.

The problem with Lucky was that he just could not stay out of trouble. What's worse, he always got caught. That's where the name Lucky came from. When Lucky was out on liberty and drinking, he was always getting into some kind of shit. He either did not make it back on time, or got in a fight, or was dragged back aboard kicking and screaming by the shore patrol.

As a consequence, he had been restricted to the ship during the times when we were at some of the really great liberty ports.

Lucky had never been ashore in Olongapo. The poor bastard had heard all the crew raving about what a great place it was, and about the girls. This was going to be his last chance to see it, but as usual, he was restricted. Well, old Lucky decided that being restricted was not going to stop him. He'd be damned if he was going to miss seeing Olongapo.

He paid a guy who had duty to let him use his I.D. card. Lucky's card had been confiscated when he was restricted to the ship. He figured, shit, the I.D. photos were all taken in boot camp. They had lousy pictures, nobody had any hair, and you pretty much couldn't tell one from the other. Then he waited until after dark, got into his civvies, snuck up to the bow of the ship, and went down the mooring line hand-over-hand to the dock. The I.D. card worked perfectly. The Marine guard waved him right through the gate.

Well, Lucky was playing catch up, so he started drinking heavy right away. While he was still able, he picked himself a girl from whatever bar he was drinking in and they got a room in the short time hotel next door. Lucky brought a bottle with him and was still drinking in the room. He undressed and climbed into bed. He told the girl to get herself ready, that he was just going to close his eyes for a minute.

She said, "Okay Joe, I just go to bathroom."

"Yeah," Lucky said, "Wake me when you're ready."

The next thing Lucky heard was the door slamming. He looked around and the girl was gone. So were his clothes, his wallet, and his shoes. He jumped out of bed and gave chase.

He scampered out the front door of the hotel, bare-assed naked, just in time to see her disappear around a corner into the 'off limits neighborhood'. Lucky hollered at her and followed her into the off limits area, almost knocking down a shore patrolman in his haste.

So, picture this; a hooker with an armload of clothes being chased by a naked sailor who was being chased now by several shore patrolmen. Well, the girl gave him the slip, no sweat, and he figured he was fucked. He dived under a parked bus to try and hide from the shore patrol. That's where they found him. They pulled him out, took him back to the base, and put him in the front gate brig and called the ship to have someone come and get him.

Lucky lost a stripe on that escapade and had his restriction aboard extended. Poor bastard, we really couldn't help feeling sorry for old Lucky, another *Basswood* living legend.

I wasn't too proud of my last performance in Olongapo either. I hate sad goodbyes, so when I got to the Coconut Grove I walked right past Mari Sol and hooked up with this little eighteen-year-old sex machine. I'll never forget the really disappointed look in Mari Sol's eyes that day as I walked out of the bar with the new girl. Yeah, I felt like a real shit heel. But damn it, she was hot and, if a girl in every port is okay, why not more than one or several?

We took off the next morning for Vung Tau Harbor in the Republic of Vietnam. There were a bunch of us on the fantail as we sailed away, giving a fond farewell to Subic Bay and Olongapo as they disappeared in our wake.

21 VIETNAM MISSION ~ VUNG TAU

In order to understand the Coast Guard's A to N mission in Vietnam, you have to understand a little something about the geography of Southeast Asia, and the countries there whose tributary rivers feed the mighty Mekong Delta. A lot of the commerce in these countries takes place on navigable waterways, in particular, Thailand and Vietnam. In Vietnam, waterways provide more opportunities for commerce and transportation than roads do.

Many of the rivers were treacherous to navigate with fast currents and tricky tides. They had dangerous curves, shifting sandy bottoms, and many obstructions. American forces also used these waterways in the Vietnam War effort. And the old French A to N system was outdated and in disrepair. Without an accurate, up-to-date system of buoys and channel markers, you could find yourself aground on a shifting sand bar or holed on an unmarked, submerged obstacle or in the wrong channel coming around a tight bend in the river. Our job, and those of the other Coast Guard buoy tenders deployed to Vietnam, was to rebuild the old French system.

Part of the job was to remove the old, mostly non-functioning French gas-powered buoys and replace them with modern battery-powered ones. We placed sea buoys at the entrances to sea ports and channel buoys to mark shipping lanes in and out of the harbors. We placed wreck and obstacle buoys where we found them. We went in the larger navigable rivers and replaced and repaired shore aids like day boards and other permanently mounted channel markers as well as river channel buoys and light houses.

Much of this work required sending work parties ashore in some pretty dangerous places. Muddy slippery areas, overgrown mangrove swamps and jungle, and in many instances, hostile territory. The hostile areas were the original reason for sending the Navy SEALS along with us. Now, we would be working missions together, their missions and our missions, and in one case a combined-mission that no one expected.

We arrived in Cat Lo on Thanksgiving Day. The next day a meeting was held with the local SEAL Command and our CO. They wanted to see how some of their operations would dovetail with our schedule of work in the bays and rivers. Then they assigned missions to the on board SEAL Team accordingly. Due to time constraints involving a couple of the workable SEAL missions, we were going to alter our A to N work. We had planned to work the Vung Tau Harbor and then go up the Saigon River as far as Saigon. Then return to the coast and work our way north. Instead, we were going north up past Da Nang to Hue and would work our way back to Vung Tau.

Working a large buoy like a harbor sea buoy is a big job and requires a coordinated team effort.

After locating the buoy we intended to wok, the bridge crew takes a fix on it to make sure it's where it is supposed to be. Then, the ship pulls alongside the buoy and the deck force hooks the boom to the lifting ring. It is then lifted out of the water and over the buoy deck. At the same time, other crewmen use chain tongs (steel hooks with a tee handle) to guide the buoy's anchor chain into the chain stopper. A heavy piece of steel with a U-shaped notch in it where the chain link will fit. A buoy anchor is a large square piece of reinforced concrete with a large ring bolt on top for hooking up to the anchor chain.

Once the buoy is in the proper position and secured on deck, the deck force goes to work on it. There are several activities going on at once. Some of the crewmen are scraping the barnacles, other shell fish, and old paint off of the bottom and inside the buoy tube (counter balance to keep buoy sanding upright when it's in the water). Others are cutting off the old shackles with a cutting torch and replacing them with new ones which they heat red hot and pound closed with sledge hammers. While still other crewmen are unbolting the two covers on the top of the buoy and removing the old battery racks and putting new ones in place. The lamp and wiring are checked and replaced or repaired as needed. Then the buoy is repainted with quick drying paint.

When it's ready to go back in the water, they use the main boom and the vang (auxiliary cable hoist) and the buoy anchor is lifted completely out of the water and held in place by the chain stopper. Meanwhile, the chain is faked out on deck in an orderly fashion and tied off with light line so when the sinker is released it will play out over the side in an orderly and smooth fashion. The captain then maneuvers the ship back to the proper coordinates.

When the ship is in position, the signal is giving and the chain stopper is released, letting the buoy follow the chain over the side of the ship and back into the water.

I may have skipped a few steps in the process, in fact, I'm sure I did, but you can see that this is a complex and dangerous undertaking. And I might add here that the weather and sea conditions do not always cooperate, making it even more dangerous. All the information about these aids, kind of buoy, type of marker (reason) and the navigational coordinates and so on, are logged and the information is forwarded to the international maritime community. They will put it out to skippers around the world in the form of a Notice to Mariners. This way the onboard navigators can annotate their charts with the updated information.

This is just one of the many functions the Coast Guard had in Vietnam. Over 8,000 Coast Guardsmen served in Vietnam. There were usually about 1,100 coasties in country at any given time. We manned the twenty-six 82-foot Coast Guard patrol boats that made up Squadron One as well as Destroyer-sized cutters patrolling off shore in Squadron Three. The Coast Guard supplied hazardous cargo handlers at all the ports where ordnance was offloaded. Many of our people who had experience with small boats and interdiction operations also served as advisors with the RVN Junk Navy. We also manned four LORAN Stations, two in country and two in Thailand and several small A to N ships like ours. And now it looked like we we're going to be working with the Navy SEALS.

Well, that was fine with us. We were small and uncomplicated. The Coast Guard has always been a handy little service with skill sets that could often not be found in the larger services. Our motto 'Semper Paratus' is loosely translated 'Always Ready' and we were.

Vung Tau turned out to be an interesting place and just a little dangerous. It has been coined as the French Rivera of the Orient. I guess it pretty much fit that description, but I would have liked to have been visiting there in more peaceful times. There was French architecture, beaches, alfresco cafes and lots of bars. It was also an in country R & R stop for both sides. You never knew when you might be elbowing up to the bar alongside your enemy.

We tied up at an RVN Naval base that everybody used. It was in Cat Lo which is at the base of Vung Tau Harbor located near the mouth of the Saigon River. There was a lot of military there; Navy PBRs and swift boats, Coast Guard 82' patrol boats of Squadron One Division 13, all kinds of Vietnamese military. We even ran into some Australian Marines. We were there for three days, so we got to look around and tip a few with the Aussies.

Since it was Turkey Day, the cook had fixed a big meal with all the trimmings. We all stayed aboard to enjoy it. After that, me and Guns and a half dozen other guys took off to see what there was to do. We were walking past some kind of a supply warehouse on the RVN base when we came upon a bunch of Aussie Marines. They had a bucket brigade going and were passing cases of beer from the warehouse and loading them onto a lorry parked nearby. We stopped to say hello and told them we were U.S. Coast Guard (we were in civvies).

Guns asked, "What are you diggers up to?"

"Give us a hand with this beer Yank, and we'll 'shout you and your mates a cold one' over at our compound."

So, we got in line and to the refrains of Waltzing Matilda, we loaded up the lorry and took off. I don't know who we were stealing the beer from.

The Aussies had a building in a small fenced compound in one back corner of the base. We cracked open the beer and were drinking and having a good old time when I hear someone in a decidedly Yankee accent holler, "Fuck the Queen!" Then, all hell broke loose.

I think it was all pretty good natured as brawls go. Nobody got hurt real bad and I think I heard some laughing while it was going on. I managed to sneak out with only a few bumps and bruises. I got me one of those neat Aussie bush hats for my trouble. And that was just day one.

The next day Guns and I made it all the way into Vung Tau. We found a bar that looked pretty good. It had a couple of tables outside and maybe twenty tables inside. The place was about half full. It was a deep room, maybe sixty feet from the front door to the bar which ran across the left two-thirds of the back wall. Where the bar ended, there was a passageway to the heads.

We had just arrived at the bar when Guns said, "I've got to go pump my bilges."

I said, "Okay, I'll order us a drink. You want me to see if they can make you a Brave Bull?"

"Sure, that'll be great, if they can't just get me a rum and Coke."

Guns went off to the head and our drinks arrived. I had just taken one sip when the whole world blew up. The pressure wave from the blast threw me up against the bar and cracked a couple of my ribs. I was just getting to my feet when Guns came running out of the head, eyes as big as saucers, and the front of his clothes wet with piss.

"What the fuck happened?"

I could barely hear him. We looked towards the front of the building. It was pretty much gone and there were people lying all over the place, some dead, others badly wounded. I went to work and did what I could with cloth napkins and tablecloths. I tried to stop bleeding and treat folks for shock until help arrived, which, with all the military around, didn't take long.

According to the military police, a sapper was casing the bars along the street looking for a good one to throw his satchel bomb into. When the MPs spotted him, he panicked, and used our bar as a target of opportunity. The satchel charge hit the door jamb when he threw it, and didn't go inside, or we would have all bought the farm. The sapper was laying down the street bleeding out through a whole bunch of bullet holes. My ears were ringing for the next forty-eight hours. The last day in port we just stayed on the ship. We'd had enough excitement in Vung Tau.

Hey, we did have a little humor related to Vung Tau. Three of the harbor buoys were out, unlighted, and we did not have time to fix them right, so we hot packed them. A hot pack is a battery that is packed in an olive drab canvas container with straps to tie it to the buoy cage. There are some wires that come twisting out of the top and connect to the buoy light to keep it working until we can return and fix it right.

We had hot packed the three buoys and were about four hours out of Vung Tau heading north when we got a radio message that another group of SEALS had disarmed the bombs on our buoys. Well hey, I guess they could have looked like bombs. But who in the hell would want to blow the light cage off a buoy in the middle of a harbor?

Humor is where you find it. The next stop will be north of Da Nang, right outside of Hue (Whey) City.

22 IN THE RIVERS AND BAYS

We had our SEALS all tucked into various berthing areas and their gear was stowed. We had several days of steaming north up the coast of South Vietnam before we reached our first stop. It would give the SEALS and our crew some time to get used to each other. Not that I thought a lot of bonding was going to take place between our work-a-day sailors and these intense special forces hunter-killer types, but you could never tell.

In the Coast Guard, we considered ourselves to be an elite force of a sort. We are the smallest of the armed services. Back in the day, we had to get a ten percent better score on the AFQT (Armed Forces Qualification Test) than the other services to even get into the Coast Guard. We could not be color blind and we had to be able to swim. When I joined in 1957, we had thirteen weeks of boot training every bit as rigorous as the Marine Corps of the day. We were also highly specialized. Most Coast Guardsmen held a primary specialty and one or two advanced or sub-specialties. On the smaller units, we cross-trained to do each other's jobs.

One day I would be treating an injured crewmember applying a dressing to a wound. The next day I may be standing a bridge watch, supervising a shore party, or manning a machine gun.

All the SEALS were in their mid- to late- twenties and had hard ropy muscles. Not the kind that gym rats develop, but the kind you get from calisthenics, miles of swimming and running, and many hours of martial arts. If nothing else, their dress was off-putting. They wore tigerstripe BDUs with sleeves and legs cut off, boonie hats, and canvas combat boots. The tigerstripe BDUs were not issue for U.S. troops. They were a South Vietnamese camouflage pattern, and they must have had them custom made.

The only insignia they wore on this abbreviated uniform was the subdued Trident Patch of the Navy SEALS, or as it is nicknamed, the Burgermeister. Each man carried his own preferred personal sidearm, a Colt Gold Cup or a Colt Cobra, etc. They each also carried a combination fighting/diving knife. You just didn't want to mess with these guys.

The commander of this team was Lieutenant Lucien Powers II. His friends called him Luke. He was from a wealthy banking family in Connecticut. He was six one, weighed about 180, had dark hair and light blue eyes that could look right through you. His was referred to by his men as LT or Loot.

BM1 "Pounder" (for ground pounder) was an ex-Army infantryman, went airborne, served two tours in Nam, got out, joined the Navy and made the Teams. He was six four, weighed about 220 and was a Nebraska farm boy. Go figure.

QM1 Bill Ranger or "Surfer" was from the beaches of Southern California. He was blonde, about six even, and weighed about 170.

He had surfer's knots on his knees and the tops of his ankles, and various scars from coral reefs and barnacle-encrusted pilings.

RM2 "Sparky" or Midget, was the smallest at about five six. He weighed in at about 140 and was from the Oregon Coast. Sparky was built like a marathon runner who had not neglected his upper body.

When Guns and I got to know them, they turned out to be fairly regular guys, who for whatever reason chose to take it to a higher level of human endeavor. Some of the shit they did was nuts, but we still found that we could have a good time with them. Guns and I seemed to hit it off pretty well with the non-com SEALS who were petty officers like us. Maybe, it was because Guns was a weapons expert, ex-Navy, and could speak their language and I was a long-time diver and SCUBA qualified. Whatever, they were interesting guys.

More than likely, they had heard some of the liberty stories about us and wanted to find out if they were true. The SEALS spent a lot of time checking and rechecking their gear, did some exercises, and then spent the rest of the time hanging out on the fantail with Guns and I.

The rest of the crew used their off-time on the mess deck fussing with the new stereo gear they had purchased at the Air Force Exchange in Guam. They also stayed up on deck, with their fancy new SLR cameras, which we had all bought on Guam, trying to get a picture of an LBGB (little bitty gook boat). The mess deck was a little hard to take when there were three or four different rock songs playing at the same time. The fantail was much more peaceful.

"So, Guns," Pounder said, "I see you and the Doc here survived Vung Tau. What is it with you guys? We've been hearing about some of your other liberty escapades. What are you two, trouble magnets?"

"No, not at all Pounder, Doc and I have such a good time on liberty that others just naturally want to join in."

"Yeah, but does it always have to be painful?"

"You'll have to ask Doc about that. I don't have a scratch on me."

"Hey, it's just been good clean fun. Well, except maybe for that bomb the other day."

"Doc, I hope none of your guys went in that tent skivvy house just outside the RVN Navy Base," Surfer said.

"I was warned about it and I passed the word to the crew that they had a particularly virulent strain of clap happening there. I told them to keep it in their pants. However, I was standing here on the fantail the other day and saw one of my guys going in there. I expect to see him in sick bay almost anytime now."

Guns said, "We didn't figure we were going to have a real good time here, but the liberty sucks a big one. If the people don't kill you, the VD will. We're used to a more refined way of getting laid than you guys here in the Nam. No long lines, a gentler strain of clap, and friendly people who just want your money, not your blood."

"You know what they say Guns, war is hell," Pounder said.

"And this is one of those wars where the people who are supposed to be your friends look just like the enemy. Sometimes they're the same people," Surfer added.

Doc said, "Shit, I've got missing teeth, bone splinters coming out of the roof of my mouth, a newly healed broken nose, and taped ribs and I haven't even been to war yet."

Everybody cracked up.

And Pounder said, "Stick with us Doc, and maybe we can find one for you."

"Thanks, but no thanks guys. I can get fucked up enough on liberty."

Just then, the sailor I saw going into the Skivvy House outside the RVN Base came up and whispered in my ear, "Doc I need to see you in sick bay."

No matter what you tell these guys you are going to get some who don't listen. In some cases, a lot who don't listen. Before we left on this patrol, I gave my standard VD talk to the crew. I usually repeated it before we pulled into each liberty port. One, condoms are available in sick bay. Two, use them. Failing that, as soon as you pull out, take a piss and then wash with soap and water, or if nothing else just water or at least just take a piss.

Some must have listened because other than a few cases of treatable Neisseria Gonorrhea (clap) and some mechanized dandruff (Crabs), my boys were VD free. And that in and of itself, was a minor miracle considering the number of liberty ports we called on and the living conditions aboard our small ship, packed together like we were without much water for bathing.

Speaking of living conditions, our transit north up the coast was just offshore, so we had to run a darkened ship at night. That meant everything closed tight with only red light inside. You may recall our ship was not air conditioned. Inside under a darkened ship, it was pretty unbearable. My solution was a folding aluminum camp cot.

I would set it up on the fantail and tie it to a stanchion so it would not slip over the side if the weather picked up overnight. That's where I slept.

We were en route to the vicinity of Hue (Whey) City, to Tan My located at the mouth of the Huong Giang or Perfume River, which was about 500 miles. We would get there on the 27th or 28th. There was a lot of buildup going on there to support our troops fighting in I Corps.

The Navy river forces were playing catch up in the area and would not be fully operational until January of 1968, which was right around the corner. The Coast Guard was also adding to its LORAN chain and would be operating a new station at Tan My by early 1969. So, there were things that both services were interested in there. We had several days of work to do and the SEALS had several RECON operations to conduct up the river.

There was no liberty here. We went about our work. The SEALS returned quietly alongside the ship our last night there and put their gear aboard. They apparently got the information that they needed. While the non-coms cleaned and stowed their gear, the lieutenant went up to the bridge and fired off an encrypted message to his superiors.

We left the next morning, December 3rd, for the short trip south to Da Nang. Da Nang was the home port for eight 82' Coast Guard patrol boats that made up Squadron One Division 12. We didn't have a lot of work to do, but it was a big Navy and Marine base so we stayed two nights and the skipper granted port and starboard liberty.

Stateside and in non-combat areas, we would have several liberty sections and just enough people left on board to get the ship underway in an emergency.

In the war zone, half the crew always stayed aboard. In an emergency here, you would not only have to get underway, but may also have to defend the ship.

There were not many of the crew who even bothered to go ashore in Da Nang. Guns and I and the two first class SEALS went just for a look see and to buy me a birthday drink. I had just turned twenty-eight. First, we went to the Navy EM Club. The SEALS were in their normal cut-off BDUs with personal sidearms. Guns and I were in our dungarees. The SEALS walked right in.

The shore patrol at the door tapped me on the shoulder and said, "Just a minute Doc. We'll to have to hold those scissors until you leave."

I wore my bandage scissors in a scabbard on my belt. Shit, the scissors didn't even have sharp points. Go figure, but I don't blame him.

He was just trying to do his job. At least he was smart enough not to try and get the SEALS to give up their weapons. That would have been fun to watch or maybe not.

One of the SEALS said, "Shit Doc, your reputation must have preceded you. Shore patrol took your scissors, huh?"

Well, it was your typical animal farm, so we had a beer and then decided to go into town and look around. Once again, we ended up in a skivvy house. It had a bar, so we had a few drinks, kidded around with some of the girls, and then went back to the ship. Next stop was Cam Rahn Bay.

Cam Rahn was a large deep bay and it is where a lot of the ordnance and war materials came in country. There were Coast Guard hazardous cargo specialists stationed here to supervise the off-loading of the dangerous stuff.

We had several large harbor buoys to work here. We were going to start that and then drop the hook overnight. The SEALS asked us if we could anchor just inside the mouth of bay on the opposite side from the base. There was something nearby that the SEALS were interested in. It got dark and POOF, they were gone.

They never talked about their missions, but the third night out there was a big fire fight that took place somewhere over in the direction the SEALS were headed when they left the ship.

Red tracers (ours) and green tracers (theirs), some grenades going off, and then finally a cobra gunship showed up and hosed the whole area down with its mini-gun. The SEALS showed up a few hours later, none the worse for wear. Same drill as before, clean, and stow their gear and the LT goes to the bridge to send his traffic. And now we're off for Qui Nhon.

Qui Nhon was a large logistics support depot for all the troops in Northern II Corps. It was run by the U.S. Army. We also had some harbor buoys to work there. The SEALS had no mission here so some of us decided to go ashore for a drink. We were anchored out and had to take one of the ship's 26' small boats in.

As we were nearing the pier, we heard rifle reports and looked up to see a security guard with his rifle up and firing in our direction. Our first class bosun, who was operating the liberty boat, hollered, "Cease firing, you stupid fucking idiot, we're Americans."

When we got tied up and on the dock, an Army PFC with an M-14 said, "Sorry guys, I didn't know who you were."

Surfer said, "What was it that confused you, our light skin, the round eyes, our loud Hawaiian shirts, or maybe it was that great big American flag on the bow of our boat?"

"Well, you can't be too careful out here, but when I heard someone yelling 'you stupid fucking idiot,' it sounded just like my company commander in boot camp. Right then I knew you all must have been Americans."

Who could argue with that? We all just shook our heads and shuffled off to try and find somewhere to get a drink. We found a Mendel Rivers Beer Club, tipped a few, and went back to the ship. You just can't find good liberty in a war zone.

When we finished our work here, we would be heading back to Vung Tau. We had a great deal of work to do there and then up the Saigon River. It looked like we would spend Christmas day tied up at Cat Lo. It might have been Merry Christmas, but there was no silent night for some poor guys. I stood in the port air castle the evening of December 25th gnawing on a turkey drumstick from the big holiday meal Bobby Green had fixed. As we ate, we watched a firefight way off across the river. And once again, I was glad I was in the Coast Guard and not a ground pounder.

We did our work changing out all the harbor buoys and channel markers in the bay and the mouth of the river. This took us through the first week of January and into the New Year. Happy 1968. Now we were headed up the Saigon River with lots of work to do there.

It was a main shipping tributary. It consisted of roughly forty-five miles of dirty brown water from the mouth of the river to Saigon. It was a twisting serpentine river with many bends and numerous tributaries feeding into it. Much of it was bordered by the Rung Sat Special Zone (thousands of square mile of mangrove swamps). These were infested with pirates and smugglers. The whole area was a major infiltration route for the Viet Cong and North Vietnamese.

Along the river, you would find every kind of small shanty town and fishing village. Many of them were crammed side by side. They were all built up on tall stilts because of river tides. Some of the fishing villages had large fish traps running far out into the river. In other places, the jungle and swamps came right down to the river's edge. In some of these areas, farmers had burned down a couple of hectares of jungle to free up a patch of arable land. All they needed was just enough room to put up their hooch and plant a small rice field to try and eke out a living for their families.

There were boats of every kind, big and small, canoes that were poled or propelled by a long sweep oar, fishing boats with the one cylinder engines that made a 'ka chug, ka chug, ka chug' sound as they cruised along. There were also large native barges and ferries. The one common thing about the Vietnamese boats was that they all had eyes painted on each side of the bow. To ward off evil spirits, I suppose. All in all, it was a colorful place

We were in our third week of January and well up the river. The routine had been working well. The SEALS would scout the areas where we were going to work during the day and do their work at night catching sleep between missions and whenever they could.

Like I said, the SEALS didn't discuss their operations with us, but they did mention that they had noticed some unusual pockets of enemy build up, some in places you would not ordinarily expect to find them in such large numbers. The SEALS were wondering if the communists might be planning something for Tet, the Vietnamese lunar New Year, which this year started on January 30th. They said if that happened there would probably be a major shit storm throughout the country. It was sure something to think about.

23 THE RESCUE

It was a bright early morning on Monday, the last week of January. We had the ship anchored close to the north shore of the river. The SEALS were standing protection for our work detail. They were working a shore aid where the jungle came pretty much right down to the beach not far from where the ship was located.

The bridge crew heard a mayday come over the emergency radio channel from a damaged American aircraft. According to the pilot's coordinates, he was in our area heading in our direction. It was a Navy F4 Phantom. They had taken a rocket near-miss, the plane was badly damaged, and his EWO (Electronics and Weapons Officer) was seriously injured from the shrapnel that had damaged the right wing and fuselage of the aircraft.

They could not make it back to their carrier. If they did, they would not be able to land. He had just been trying to keep the plane in the air long enough to find an Allied air base or other safe place to put the plane down.

They had lost a lot of altitude and the pilot reported that they were taking small arms ground fire from a large enemy force. He was going to try and get as many miles ahead of the main force as possible, and then bail out while they still could.

Just a few minutes later, the *Basswood* bridge crew spotted the low flying fighter/bomber off to the north about five miles coming up from the east. It was flying low and trailing smoke. Our radio crew told them where to look, so they could locate our ship in relation to their position and pick out some landmarks on the ground that would help us find them once they were down. They were just slightly past our position when the canopy blew off the jet, Soon, two parachutes deployed.

While this was going on, we had recalled our work detail and the SEALS. The captain had also ordered Guns to prepare and arm some additional crewmen to accompany and assist the SEALS on a mission to rescue the downed pilots. By the time the shore party had returned to the ship, Guns and I and Seamen Jackson Randy and Montana Horton were already dressed in some of Guns' new olive drab BDUs with flak jackets and boonie hats. I had my medical pack and IV fluids and a collapsible canvas liter. We all had 1911 1A .45 caliber side arms.

The pilot landed okay but his EWO snagged his foot in the crotch of a tree and he thought his leg in broken.

He also said he had spotted what he thought were pretty good landmarks on the way down in the chute. "We're about five clicks (about three miles) nearly straight out from your ship. We're in pretty heavy jungle, but there is a cleared area with a rice field and a hooch about three clicks from us between our location and the river. There looks to be a fairly well used trail at the end of the rice paddy opposite the hooch and then through the jungle on out to the river.

"And hurry guys, I saw an advance party of about a dozen that broke off from the enemy main force and started jogging in our direction. They're still a long ways away, but they were coming fast. They will be at our location in maybe three hours."

When the SEALS were back aboard, we briefed them on what was happening. As you might expect, they were quick studies. It all got put together in triple time.

Guns said, "I picked these two seamen because they're the best, I've got on a .50 caliber."

Pounder asked how're you going to use your .50 cal on the beach.

"I've got a ground mount for it," Guns responded.

"Semper fucking Paratus," Surfer said. "Of course you do."

"I'm not trying to tell you guy's your business, but I figured that with a couple of your guys with one of your M-60s and my .50, we could set up an ambush on the trail someplace between where the downed pilots are located and the beach. That way if we have bad guys chasing us, we can run them right into our ambush. And one last thing, maybe it would be a good idea for the loaders on the crew served weapons, to each bring an M-79 Grenade Launcher."

"That sounds like a pretty good plan so far, Guns," LT Powers said. "A good place for the ambush would be right where the trail comes off this side of the rice field. When our guys come through carrying the litter, if any bad guys are following them, just lay down a barrage of automatic weapons fire and launch a few RPGs. After the litter is through to the beach, you guys can pick up your gear and *didi* out of there. What do you think, Pounder?"

"It sounds pretty good, Loot. You and I and Doc and Guns will go get the pilots. The uninjured pilot and three of us will carry the litter, and the extra guy will cover our rear."

Guns spoke up, "I think that should be me, since I'm the oldest and the smallest. I won't be much help carrying the litter. I think I would be more help with this." Guns reached behind him from a chair seat out of sight and lifted a mint condition .45 caliber Thompson submachine gun. "I've always loved these," he said, "a fully automatic weapon with real stopping power."

93

Pounder just shook his head, grinned, and said "Only in the fucking Coast Guard."

The SEALS switched to full BDUs and passed around some face paint.

LT Powers said, "Skipper, how about we use both the skimmer and your whaler, as well? It doesn't matter that it's white we're not in stealth mode out here on the river in daylight. And if you could provide a coxswain for our boat as well, it will free up all my guys for the shore mission."

"Pounder, you mount the other M60 on the skimmer and put Surfer and Sparky on the ambush M60. Give them an M79, as well. The rest of us will carry Stoners (5.56 MM light-machine gun) and side arms. After the boats drop us off, they will return and wait behind the ship. When we are on the way out and getting near the river, we will fire a green flare and you'll haul ass back to get us. We'll put the pilots, Doc and any wounded on the skipper's boat. We'll cover their exit and then the rest of us will take the skimmer back. If there are no questions, let's move."

While this was going on, the uninjured pilot had performed what first aid he could to his EWO, and then drug him as far away from their landing site as possible. After that, he cut an international orange foil survival blanket into strips and marked a trail from the southwest corner of the rice paddy trail back to where he and his wounded EWO would wait.

When the landing party came ashore, they discovered that there was a fair trail going through the jungle that was only slightly overgrown. They figured whomever had once lived in the hooch and maintained the rice field, had used it to access the river. They double-timed it until they reached the rice field.

LT Powers said, "Let's set up enfilade. Guns, have your guys move back into the jungle off the left side of the trail and set up there. Surfer, you take the right side. When we come back, we'll be humping it as fast as we can. If we're coming in hot, you'll know it, because we'll probably be returning fire. As we pass you guys, lay down a field of fire and start lobbing some RPGs into them. We'll get Doc and the pilots on their boat and then come back and help you cover your retreat to the river. If that advance group catches up with us, we can, hopefully, take them all out and get away before the main force arrives."

The LT, Guns, Pounder, and I headed up the marked trail which was not quite as easygoing as the trail to the river had been, but it was good enough, They reached the downed pilots in about an hour.

"Man, are we glad to see you guys. You almost beat me back. I guess my trail markers worked," the pilot said.

"They worked great," Powers responded.

"Okay good, now we're going to have to hustle," the pilot said, "at times I can hear the advance party. They're not making any secret that they are there and coming fast, but I don't think they have a clue about you guys."

I went straight to the injured EWO. "How you doin', Lieutenant?"

"I've been better. I think my lower leg is broken, and I've got a piece of my airplane in my chest."

I asked the pilot what he had done for his EWO and was told that he had given him a morphine syrette about an hour and fifteen minutes ago. He had put a battle dressing on the wound in the side of his chest and he had strapped his legs together while he was moving him.

"How's your pain now?" I asked.

"Not bad."

"If it starts to get worse, let me know, and I'll give you another shot."

I checked his pulse and blood pressure, started an I.V. and then put a blow up plastic splint on his broken leg. After that, I checked and redressed the chest wound with a compress and pressure dressing.

"Okay, were good to go, let's get him on the litter and get moving."

Everybody except Guns took a handle of the litter. He took the rear of the column and they left at a quick walk. By then, we could all hear the enemy crashing through the jungle, but still a ways off. We were about two clicks from ambush site, when we had first contact with the advance force. Some wild rounds were fired at them by their pursuers while they were still some distance away.

Guns had also decided to bring an M79 and he fired off an RPG at them and fired a full thirty-round magazine through his Thompson to slow them down a little. Then he caught up with the litter bearers, who were now almost running.

Before the enemy had recouped and caught up with us again, we were past the ambush site. We were down the easier trail a fair distance when we heard the machine guns light off and then some more RPGs. When the litter reached the river, we did not have to signal the boats. They had heard the weapons fire and were almost there.

The LT and Pounder headed back to help the guys on the machine guns extract themselves. When the skipper's gig arrived, the pilot and I loaded the EWO and headed back to the ship. By the time the two

SEALS arrived back at the ambush site, the firing was intermittent, and they figured a good number of the enemy must be down.

The LT said, "Let's wait a bit and then when it's all clear, we'll make a break for the beach."

After a few minutes with no action he instructed the M60 crew to head out. Then he told the .50 caliber crew to get ready to go and he and Pounder headed down the trail.

Montana got up, picked up two cans of ammo, and turned and headed down the trail. He hollered back at Randy, "Come on, grab the gun and lets go!" and kept on walking.

Just before Randy picked up to go, the last six Viet Cong soldiers busted out of the jungle and rushed the machine gun in a suicide attack.

Randy said to himself, "Oh shit," and opened fire. He killed three of the attackers before he took a round in the forehead, killing him instantly.

Montana did not see Jackson behind him, and then he heard the gunfire.

He hollered to Pounder, "My buddy's in trouble. I'm going back."

When he rounded the bend in the trail, he saw that Jackson was down. He ran towards the .50 cal and his buddy, emptying his .45 pistol at the enemy on the way. He hoisted Jackson on his right shoulder and picked up the fifty in his left hand, turned and started back down the trail. Just as Pounder showed up, a round hit Montana on the left side of his neck, but he just kept going as Pounder opened up with his stoner. He kept firing his weapon while backing away and covering Montana's rear. When the two Coasties had rounded a bend in the trail, Pounder turned and ran after them. As he did, one of the dying VC got off a last round that hit Pounder in his left side just above the hip, where his love handles would have been, if he'd had love handles. He just grunted and kept running.

As they neared the river, the skimmer pulled to one side and covered their retreat with the M60. Surfer was firing RPGs as quick as he could load the M79. We put Jackson and the two wounded in the skipper's gig, which had also returned. The others jumped in the skimmer. We all headed for the port side of the ship. As soon as the small craft were under the ship's guns, the two starboard .50 calibers started raking the beach.

The skipper had radioed a request for assistance and two Cobra gunships were about five minutes out. There were also a couple of Navy PBRs on the way. The skipper already had the ship underway and heading up stream when the two whalers pulled alongside. Everyone came aboard, and the whalers were loaded on deck.

Jackson was placed in a body bag and placed in the shade of the fantail awning.

The wounded were taken to sick bay for treatment. After I checked out Pounder, I told the skipper he would be okay until we arrived in Saigon where he could be evacuated to a medical treatment facility. I dressed his wound, administered some morphine, put him on an IV, and gave him a prophylactic shot of penicillin.

Montana's wound looked worse than it was. It was at the juncture of his neck and shoulder where it deeply grazed the meaty part of his trapezius muscle. I cleaned his wound and was able to close it with some heavy sutures. He would have a nice scar, but he was good to go.

To add insult to injury, we hit a sandbar three miles up the river and ran the ship aground. We were at battle stations for four hours while we got the ship refloated. It was a combination of things that got us unstuck. We transferred ballast around, moved the ship back and forth, and the tide coming in.

By luck, we had not attracted any enemy fire while we were aground. The main force had finally reached the river, just in time for the helicopters to hose them down with several passes of mini-gun and rocket fire. The Cobras returned to their base to refuel, then returned and flew cover for us until we were free of the sandbar. In the meantime, the two PBRs stood off and kept us covered.

Finally, we arrived in Saigon. There was a Navy contingent waiting to take charge of the pilots. They also took Pounder to a clinic to get patched up. We had a small service for Jackson Randy and then turned him over to graves registration.

At the clinic, Pounder had some minor surgery done to repair his wound and was back aboard two days later, just in time to head back down the river with us.

I asked him, "What's with you SEALS, you can't take a little time off when you've been shot?"

"Shit no Doc, and besides you didn't leave 'em much to do at the clinic. They poked and prodded and took some x-rays. Said the wound was clean and there didn't appear to be any infection. They just put a clean dressing on, gave me some antibiotic pills, and told me to take it easy for a week or so and not to lift anything heavy. Those little honeys in Okinawa and Taiwan aren't very heavy, are they Doc?"

"Fucking SEALS."

The skipper had given us a couple of days of Cinderella liberty in Saigon while we were waiting for supplies from Tan Son Nhut Air Base. It was not much fun, particularly after losing one of our guys. It was interesting, however, to just walk around and look. Other than the presence of quite a few armed military police, it seemed pretty much business as usual. There were European-style buildings and thousands of little cars and mini-bikes and Vietnamese girls in traditional ao dias. We wore civvies, but every other round eye we saw was in BDUs and many carried a gun of some sort.

The black market was crazy. They didn't even try to cover it up. You could buy anything from the States, usually off the pallet it arrived in country on. Uniforms, booze, skivvies, tools, combat boots. You name it, they had it. I bought myself another Aussie hat.

I lost the one from the brawl in Cat Lo when I decided to wear it during our rescue operation. I bought patches from all the places we worked in country and even an engraved Zippo lighter.

The girls were beautiful, especially the Eurasians, the half-French ones. We had a few drinks with some of them, but nobody bothered to shack up because we had to be back aboard by midnight. They all thought we were CIA, because we were not in uniform. Shit, we could have gotten in trouble there and had it blamed on the CIA. No such luck.

We got some intel back on the ship from our SEAL buddies. Apparently, that main force group we had tangled with, was massed for another purpose. It looked like the North Vietnamese were getting set for a huge offensive on the Tet Holiday, and those guys were to be part of it.

They suspected that this was going to be a county-wide offensive and that all hell would probably be breaking out everywhere. And that was only two days away.

Based on this information, the skipper made a decision. We had a little work left to do in this area and a lot of work in the Bassac River, a bad place in the best of times. We were going to shoot down the Saigon River, go finish our work in Okinawa, and then take five days R&R in Taiwan. Then, we would see how things were going with the Offensive. If it had settled down some, we would finish the Saigon River and then do the Bassac. We would be finished with our work in Vietnam.

After that, the skipper said we would go to Bangkok, Thailand for some real R&R. Everybody wanted to promote him from captain to king. Is the Coast Guard great, or what?

24 OKINAWA II AND TAIWAN

We hit the mouth of Vung Tau Bay at all ahead flank speed on 30 January 1967. When we were about three miles off shore, we turned to port, slowed down to about ten knots, and headed to Okinawa about six days away. The skipper had scheduled three days there to complete our work. It would be a nice vacation for the SEALS, and would give Pounder a chance to heal.

Okinawa was not a big draw for the crew, but at least we would not be getting shot at. And good guys that we were, we were willing to give the Japanese girls another chance. If that didn't work, there was always Taiwan a few days later and there was a lot of word going around about that place, all good. It would also be another spot for me to check off on my travel map of the world.

When we arrived in Naha, it was colder than hell.

All our civvies were of the tropical kind, so, we decided to wear Dress Blues with the new flat hats (Donald Duck hats) and pea coats. This would be the first time anyone in Okinawa had seen the new hats. We had also adopted the new practice of sewing our rate and ranking on the pea coat sleeves. The girls all thought Guns and I were chiefs. Well, first class was close, the hard hats fooled them and the coats were double breasted like a chief's blouse. We didn't mind and just played along. The only reason they cared was that they figured that chiefs had more money.

Guns and I and a few of the other guys found a new bar that looked promising. We decided to stop there for awhile and see what the girl situation looked like. It looked good and we picked out a couple of cute ones to sit with us, have a few drinks, listen to the band, and later do the horizontal mambo. Things were going along fine. We were all having a good time and were starting to rethink our attitude about Okinawa. Sailors are easy.

Later, when we felt the time was right, we ponied up the cash and checked our girls out of the bar. They took us to a small hotel where we could do the deed. We left our shoes at the door as is the custom in Japan. We checked in with the mama-san and then went to our rooms. When we got to the room, I told my girl I had to use the head. She said okay and told me she had to run down to see the mama-san and that she'd be right back.

I took care of my business, got undressed, and got into the sack. It was not really a bed but a thick futon on a mat on the floor. Then I waited, and waited. After thirty or forty minutes I thought, *what the fuck,* then I slipped on my pants and went and knocked on Guns' door.

He answered the door and said, "I think we've been fucked shipmate, and not in a good way."

"Well, that sucks," I said. "You want to go back to the bar?"

"Naw, it's late, let's go back to the ship. We'll pay them a visit tomorrow."

When we got down to the front door, our shoes were gone and we thought, *fuck, they stole our shoes too.* Then we rousted the mama-san out of bed. She took us to a cabinet and got our shoes out. She didn't know anything about the girls, of course. So, it was back to the ship for us and tomorrow would be another day.

When we returned to the ship, we told the quarter deck watch what happened, He said that we weren't alone. Another three or four guys had gotten back to the ship just before us and were complaining about the same thing. Well, we hit the sack. By the time we got up the next morning, it was all over the ship. Six other guys got taken for their fees just like we had.

Some folks don't know it, but being a small service traveling around the world on small ships, we have become like those old French musketeers, "One for all and all for one". In this case, sixty-four for eight. With three section liberty here in Okinawa, we could put twenty guys on the beach at one time. A rough plan was put together to get our money back. Everyone would wear dress blues, so that the people at the bar that had stiffed us would be sure to know who we were. We would all go about our early afternoon liberty, then muster outside the bar in question at about 7:00 p.m. that evening, and take it from there.

So, Guns and I went to look for a place to kill some time.

Only in the Orient do you find places like 'Cindy's Lounge and Steam Bath Massage'.

Guns said, "Let's try this place."

On the main floor, there was a long oval bar. We set down at one end of the oval and ordered our drinks. Then I noticed that the CO and Mr. Gunderson were sitting at the other end of the oval. I waved and said "Hi skipper, Hi Mr. Gunderson."

They waved back. Then, the skipper came down and said, "Can we join you guys? I just found a bottle of my favorite '151 proof Lemon Heart Rum. You can help us drink it."

We said, "bring it on down."

We all got settled and poured our drinks.

The skipper said, "Doc, Guns, what are you guys up to today?"

"I don't think you want to know, skipper," I responded.

"Sure I do," he said.

"Well, first we're going to drink for a bit longer. Then we're going upstairs and get a steam bath and massage." Then I told him about our forthcoming muster at the bar and the rip off.

Guns told them they were welcome to tag along if they wanted. And, they said that they just might do that. After a bit, Guns and I were ready to go up and try out the services upstairs.

They had a list of services as long as a Chinese restaurant menu. First, they stripped us down to our birthday suits. They put us in a couple of those steam boxes, where only your head sticks out. Next, they set us on little three-legged stools and scrubbed us with soap and a fairly soft brush until we were pink all over.

They give you a soft cloth and some soap and let you do your own privates. I guess they didn't want to touch us until they were sure we were clean. When that was done, they put us in a big wooden tub full of near scalding water. We soaked until we went from pink to bright red. That's when I knew what a poor lobster felt like. Guns already knew. He had had one of these sessions many times before.

After the soak was done, they dried us off and put us on the massage tables where they oiled, powdered, pummeled, pushed, yanked, twisted, stretched, and rubbed everything. When they were done with us, we had to hold on to something until our muscles came back into service again and we were able to stand un-aided. There was no buzz left from our earlier drinking so we would have to start all over. There was plenty of time for drinking later. It was about time to get our little show on the road.

As we got near to the bar in question, it looked like we had a good turnout.

The skipper said, "That looks like the whole liberty party."

"Well, they were all invited," I responded.

One of our drinking buddies, a first class quartermaster named Dan Eustis, became our nominal leader in this undertaking. Dan was a former boxer and was no one you wanted to mess with. He yanked open the front door and twenty-odd coasties filed in. All were in dress blues and flat hats except the skipper and Mr. Gunderson, who were in civvies. The crew lined up against the rear wall, arms folded across their chests, a look of resolve on their faces. Eustis jumped up on the stage and took the mike away from the band singer.

He said, "We're from the U.S. Coast Guard Cutter *Basswood*. Several of our crewmembers were swindled out of their money by this establishment yesterday. We have come to get it back for them. If you

101

don't want to get involved, I suggest that you leave in the next few minutes. After we close and lock the door it will be too late."

All the time this announcement was going on, the captain was standing beside me and mumbling. "I'm the captain, I'm the captain. I shouldn't be here."

I whispered to him, "Don't worry, I don't think they're going to take a chance getting their club trashed."

And sure enough, just as I'd said that, a short, stocky little Japanese guy with thick glasses came running out of a back office with a fist full of cash yelling, "NO, NO, we play, we play, how muchee?, we play." And he did. We had already totaled up the figure and he counted it out. The money was handed out to those of us who had been taken. Everyone filed out and went back to whatever they were doing. Those of us who had been ripped off went down the street and had a little celebratory drink before going back to the ship.

Where were the SEALS, you ask? They were not on our duty roster and had no responsibility to the ship outside of the war zone. So, they went off on their own for the whole three days and came back aboard just before we got underway to Taiwan. You just never knew what those guys were up to. They weren't telling.

It was an overnight run back down to Taiwan. We left at 1600 and would be there the next day in the late afternoon. We weren't going to Taipei or Kaohsiung, the big cities where all the tourists and other services went.

The Coast Guard's favorite port, or so I was told, was Keelung.

It was located in a more industrial part of Taiwan. It was a kind of gritty place, a merchant port. It's where the ocean-going freighters that brought in raw materials and hauled out finished products tied up. They came and went with their miscellaneous cargo and also frequented the bars and bar girls while they were there.

It looked more like I imagined old China might look like in the areas of the country where the laboring people lived and worked. No tall buildings and lots of factories both large and small with lots of open market places where you could buy almost anything before it got the tourist markup. And, you were expected to haggle for anything you bought. There were some great deals to be had. Jewelry boxes, clothes, pirated records, books out of copyright, you name it. I bought some jewelry boxes and a couple of medical books.

Of primary interest to us, of course, were lots of bars and pretty bar girls. And there was at least one good hotel. Nancy's Harbor Hotel, stood about four stories high and overlooked the harbor. As the program was explained to me, you went and found your girl for the whole stay and then rented yourself a room on the top floor of the Harbor Hotel. That's where the bar and dance floor were located, as well as a great view of the harbor. Shit, I was ready.

Guns told me that we would not need much money. We just needed to bring about a dozen cartons of cigarettes each, half Winston's and half Salem's. He said with those you should be able to get your girl for five days and two or three bank bundles of NTs (New Taiwan Dollars) enough to pay for your hotel room and other extras. It sounded good to me. The Sea Stores Cigarettes only cost me $1.10 a carton.

When we were ready to go, I packed the smokes in an AWOL bag and covered them with an old shirt. The problem was, we were tied up outboard of a Taiwanese customs ship and we were smuggling black market smokes into their country. No worry, we walked across their quarter deck going ashore and no one paid any attention to us.

We found the bar Guns was looking for, the Blue Bird. We went in and conducted our business. I left there with a heart-stopping beautiful twenty-year-old girl named Cindy. She would have made Suzy Wong look like a boy. I don't know what her real name was and I didn't care. They all adopt a first name that westerners could pronounce. Those names that start with x or y and have no vowels are tough. So it was just part of the service to make it easier for us.

As it turned out, the crew had rented the whole top floor of the hotel and we commenced a five day ship's party. Again, there were no SEALS. They were nice guys, but somehow we didn't miss them. My little gal turned out to be a really nice person. Besides sleeping with me, she showed me everything there was to see in her town. I went to the open market with her while she shopped for her mom.

They were having snake soup that day, so she had to buy a fresh *habushu* or *habu* snake, live, fresh and very poisonous. They were a member of the pit viper family of snakes. She pointed out the snake she wanted. The snake clerk reached in the cage, very fast, and snatched the snake right behind the head. Then, he took a small sharp knife, slit the skin around the head, and with his other hand popped the whole skin off. He stuck it in a paper bag and tied the top while the old snake was still thrashing around. At least you knew it was fresh.

She paid the agreed upon price and we were on our way. Snake soup, veggies, rice and Cindy. It doesn't get any better than that.

One day Cindy's mom cooked us a whole steamed chicken and sent it to the hotel for us. It did not look very appetizing; no color, looked raw, but it tasted good. I found out that I liked it when we were able to stay some place where I could be with one girl the whole time we were there. I got my ashes hauled, and also got steeped in the local culture. Like I've said before, mostly they were just kids in a third world country making a living the best way they could.

Well, it was a good port call and almost incident free. On about the third day, Guns and I were out getting some air with our girls. Hey, as hard as you may try, you can't stay in bed twenty-four hours a day. They were showing us some sights around town when we ran into Montana and one of his buddies. You remember Montana from the mix up with the VC. His shoulder wound was pretty much healed by now.

Montana was a fun guy most of the time. He was a twenty-one year old, six foot four inch, 240 pound farmer from Texas and strong as a horse. Why Montana? He was born in Montana while his father was working there. When Montana was two, his grandfather died and his folks moved back to Texas to run the family farm. Aside from the name, he was all Texan. He had ancestors who had fought in the Alamo.

He was a pretty simple guy. He was honest, a hard worker, and would back his friends to the max in a fight. When the opportunity presented itself, Montana enjoyed a good time and liked to have fun.

This day, he and his friend were riding in a couple of rickshaws. These were one step up from the old ones with a guy running between two poles. Now the poles were connected to a bicycle and they would peddle you around.

Well, the two coasties thought it would be fun to try driving these things. They put their drivers in the back of the rickshaws, borrowed their little conical coolie hats, and started peddling around town. Well, it wasn't long before they decided to see how fast they could go, and then it was a race. They were going along like a good thing running people out of the way up one street and down the next. Then, all of a sudden, they were going down a hill and picking up speed. The little Chinamen in the back were yelling and screaming.

Did I mention that in this particular town they had outdoor open sewers? In Japan, they call them *benjo* ditches (canals of human waste). I don't know what they called them in Taiwan, but there was one at the bottom of the hill and it was coming up fast. There was about a foot-high curb and then a fairly wide ditch full of shit. Montana and his buddy saw this coming and bailed off. When the front wheels of the bikes hit that curb, they came to an abrupt stop and catapulted the two Chinese drivers right into the ditch.

Everybody was still laughing about it when we went into the Blue Bird for a drink later that day. I asked, "Where is Montana?"

Andy, the other rickshaw racer said, "He's in the head."

That reminded me. I had to take a leak, so I went on back to the head myself. One other thing I might mention.

The heads here were uni-sex and that took a little getting used to for us prudish Americans. They were mostly set up with a row of sinks with mirrors on one wall with urinals or maybe a big trough for guys to pee in on the back wall. They would have a little step-up tiled or cement area at one side or the other with one or more holes about the size of a large dinner plate to squat over for the girls to pee and for everyone to do number two.

As I walked in, there were a bunch of girls at the mirrors giggling and fixing their makeup. I stepped over to the urinal and started to take a leak. I almost peed on myself when I spied Montana over to my right. He still had the coolie hat on and he had his ass screwed right down on one of those nasty holes taking a dump and drinking from a liter bottle of Chinese beer. When he saw me, he got a great big stupid grin on his face and said, "Hey Doc, look at the size of these long neckers." And, you wonder why the Chinese call us White Devils.

The only incident of any kind was due to the local curfew. It was 2000 hours, or ten o'clock and as far as the Taiwanese were concerned. They were on a war footing with mainland China. So, they were very serious about enforcing the curfew. If they caught you out after 2000, if you were lucky, they would simply march you back to your ship with a gun in your ear. And, of course, some of our guys found out about this the hard way.

The SEALS came back aboard. We had hauled the gangway in and were starting to throw off the mooring lines. Someone hollered, "Hey, look at old Boats, he's getting some on the dock." Sure enough, there was one of our boatswain's mates. He had his girl bent over an empty cable spool getting some last-minute doggy style action. He pulled out, zipped up, and ran across the Taiwanese ship's quarterdeck.

Then he made an amazing Olympic-class broad jump across the rapidly increasing space between the two ships as we were pulling away. He made a perfect landing on deck with a big-ass grin on his face and took a big bow. The SEALS were standing there watching. In chorus they said, "Fucking Coast Guard."

It would be the twenty-second or third of February by the time we got back to Vung Tau. The worst of the Tet Offensive was over, at least, where we were going. So, the skipper said, "Let's get it done." And we sailed away from Heaven and back into Hell.

25 BACK TO NAM AND THEN OFF TO R & R

We ran back up the Saigon River and worked our last couple of aids there and then straight back. We turned south at the mouth of Vung Tau Bay for the short run to the Bassac River. We spent about two weeks there and except getting a few shots plinked at us by the VC, it was uneventful. That was it, our Vietnam mission was complete. I guess it was successful by most standards of measure in a war zone. The SEALS concluded several successful operations, we got our A to N work completed, and rescued two Navy pilots with the rescue party suffering one casualty and two wounded. But, I think Jackson Randy's folks might have a different opinion about the success of our mission. I only hope that the fact that he died a hero helped to dull their pain.

Now we were headed for Thailand. First, we would pull in at Sattahip, and drop off the SEALS and their gear.

The SEALS would catch a C-130 out of Udorn Air Base back to their base and then to their next operation. After that, we would proceed up river to Bangkok and five days of R & R before heading back to the Philippines, Sangley Point, and then home to Guam.

Me and Guns and a couple of the other guys were hanging out on the fantail with the SEAL enlisted when Pounder said, "You know you just don't hear much about the Coast Guard."

"I met a couple of Coast Guard guys on the 82-foot patrol boats back in 1965 when they had just arrived in country," Surfer chimed in. "They seemed okay to me."

"We don't have much of a PR Department," Guns said.

"Well Shit, Guns, they're trying," I said. "Look at the neat Donald Duck hats they gave us with Coast Guard written right there on the hat ribbon and look at the big Coast Guard we got painted on the side of the ship. When we get back to Guam, we get to add a big red and blue racing stripe. Pretty soon everybody will know us."

"Well," Pounder said, "for what it's worth, you guys did good. You can fight next to me anytime."

"Thanks Pounder, that means a lot coming from you," Guns said.

Then together, both Surfer and Pounder said, "We just won't go on liberty with you. It's too damned dangerous, especially with Doc. A person could get hurt."

Everybody on the fantail cracked up.

A few days later they offloaded the SEALS and their gear. Everybody did biker hugs and bumped fists and said their goodbyes. They were gone and we headed up the Chao Phraya River to Bangkok.

It's not a long run, but because of the 14-knot current we had to wait for the incoming tide. It still took us over half a day to get up river to the Royal Thai Ordnance Depot in Bangna just outside Bangkok where we tied up the ship. It was a beautiful ride up the river. There were many small picturesque villages all surrounded by what appeared to be heavy jungle. Even in the smallest of these villages, you could see the colorful roofs and spires of Buddhist Temples rising above them. There were also many, many different and colorful watercraft plying the waters beside and around us. As we got closer to Bangkok, the river was busy with water taxis zipping here and there. We even got a look at the King's barge. It was like something from ancient Egypt. It was a huge gold-colored or maybe plated barge with deep red or maroon trim and canopy. I counted seventy oars on one side.

We finally got tied up and were met by the commanding officer of the ordnance depot. He welcomed us to Thailand and offered his personnel as guides for those who would like to use them. Guns and I selected a couple of guys who were the equivalent of chief petty officers. They were nice guys who could speak some English and would take nothing for their services.

There was one problem for a lot of the crew. Our pay had not caught up with us for the last couple of months. A lot of the guys were flat broke. This was actually a boon for Guns. He was the shipboard $5.00 for $10.00 guy. Every ship had one. Guns made a bundle of money because those lazy bastards at the Bangkok JSMAC Thailand did not get our pay to us until the fourth day of a five day R & R.

This did not slow Guns and I down. He had a locker full of money. I always had some cash stashed for emergencies.

I know that the shore duty pogues don't think a lot about their seagoing brethren. So, you had to be ready for instances like this. Semper Paratus. Guns took care of his loan business and we grabbed our guides and we were off to do the town. These guys also had their own wheels, which was a big plus. First they took us on a drive through town and found us a hotel. It was an American class hotel. In fact, it was even called the American Hotel.

Some of the other guys found rooms in a place called the Happy Hotel. It had one benefit that appealed to some of the young crazy guys on the crew. The second floor rooms had balconies right over the pool. You guessed it. We had some wannabe Acapulco cliff divers who decided it would be cool to enter the pool from their balconies. Somehow, they all survived.

On the trip to the hotel and around town I was glad I was not driving. It was the busiest traffic I had ever seen, including other parts of

Asia. There were, of course, trucks and buses and cars, but there were also thousands of small trucks with metal roofs over the beds used as jitneys to get people around. *Tuk Tuks*, three-wheeled motorized rickshaws, also whizzed by. Standard two-wheel scooters and motorcycles also vied for road space. Sometime, they were all packed together so close you could not have gotten a playing card between them.

They don't use breaks, but rather horns, speed, and maneuverability to avoid crashing into each other. Talk about a white-knuckle ride. Another thing I've seen in all Southeast Asia traffic, including the Philippines, Vietnam, and Thailand were whole families, five people, riding on one two-wheel motorcycle or people using them to transport freight. I saw one with eight or ten cases of Coke stacked on the back fender of a motorcycle.

On our drive through town, we noticed that they were emulating a lot of our 60's pop culture, to get the R & R business, I guess. We drove past several huge night clubs named after the current dance craze in the States. They were all named something a Go Go. Like the Whiskey a Go Go or San Francisco a Go Go. And each one had hundreds, maybe thousands of bar girls, each with their own name badge with a number on it. The Thai people were very organized, if nothing else.

After checking into our hotel rooms, our military guides took us to the Whiskey a Go Go, and we picked out a couple of beautiful gals to be our escorts for the entire stay. Our two Thai chiefs assured us that the girls would take very good care of us and could show us the whole city and all the sights around Bangkok. The guys said they would check in with us each morning at the hotel to see if we would need them or the car. What a wonderful liberty town this turned out to be.

If anything, Bangkok and its surrounds were like a huge fairy tale town. Forget Alice. To me, this was 'Sailor in Wonderland'. Even the few tokers (pot heads) we had on board, loved it there. One day as I was walking to my hotel room, I passed a couple of them in the hall.

One of them exclaimed, "What a great place," and he held up a plastic baggy of Asian Red Pot the size of a pillow case and said, "only five bucks."

I said, "Have a good time, but I don't want to see any of that shit aboard ship." Right!

I was glad we had the girls. Or, we would not have known where to go first or what to see. I don't think we missed anything including the *khlongs*, which were the many canals and tributaries off the Chao Phraya River which surrounds Bangkok.

They were a floating marketplace filled with shops on barges, and boats in the canals, as well as along the shores. If Vung Tau was the French Riviera of the East the *khlongs* in Thailand were the Venice of the East.

The girls took us to the small shops where craftsmen could make you a ring or other jewelry from scratch and have it finished before your R & R was over. The most popular of these were gold rings with a single cat's eye, sapphire mounted on it. All of these shops would serve you a glass of Singha Thai beer while you shopped, whether you bought anything or not.

They also took us to TIM Land or Thai in Miniature Land, where we spent one whole day. It was a huge exhibit. It had a jungle area along a river where you could watch Indian elephants pick up, move, and place giant teak logs in the river. Indian elephants are smaller than the African variety, but boy, can they work.

There was an auditorium where you could watch beautiful girls perform all the traditional Thai dances. The colorful costumes, the music, and the many movements and positions these dancers could put their bodies through and into, was almost hypnotic.

After that, we went to a covered outdoor arena where several presentations were made. Thai sword fighting was so fast the contestants were, at times, a blur as the blades clanged and sparks flew off them. One misstep and someone could lose an arm or a head. After that, we saw bloodless Thai cockfighting. They used no spurs and fought only until one cock ran away and would fight no more. Following the cockfight, they demonstrated force-feeding a huge python snake.

Then, we went to an indoor arena and watched several bouts of Muay Thai or Thai boxing. If I thought the sword fighting was fast, I had seen nothing yet. Even with 400-speed film in my camera, some of my pictures came out as just a blurry outline of the action. These are the guys who challenge Chinese *Kung Fu* fighters to an annual match and routinely kick their asses.

The final events at TIM Land that we watched was a snake handler wading through a pit of cobras all standing up with their hoods flared. The snake handler moved them around with a snake hook without getting bitten. Then, there was a photo opportunity with one of their very large pythons wrapped around your shoulders. I opted out of that one.

After that we went back to town and ate all the best stuff the street vendors could offer. Other times we ate at regular Thai restaurants or ordered in at the Hotel. I learned about the hot Thai food the hard way. Hey, I'd had plenty of Mexican food and Korean food and I didn't think hot bothered me. My mistake. One of the first meals I ate had been sprinkled with what I thought were sliced green onion tops and I took a big mouth full. They were little, hot green peppers. Jesus, I think I got third-degree burns on my tongue.

The next day we took a water taxi tour among the *khlongs* and then went on to look at many of the different Buddhist temples including the Golden Buddha, the Reclining Buddha, and the Temple of Dawn. If Dawn is not one of the eight wonders of the world, it should be. I was able to climb the outside of the temple and get photos of most of Bangkok as well as the *khlongs*.

In Bangkok, and I guess pretty much all Thailand there are many, many temples. They even have small temples along the roadways, in case someone has a prayer that just can't wait.

There are also little shrines with the figure of a man's erect phallus where women who want to get pregnant can pray. I thought it might be a good idea to hang around one to see if any of the gals needed help with that project.

After all of this exercise we needed, you guessed it, a massage. The girls took us to a large massage parlor. Once again, beer was served while we picked out our masseuse. To do this, they handed you a program book. It had a picture of each girl and a short biography with her name, age, height, weight, education, languages spoken, and home province. There was also a number that corresponded to the badge she wore.

To view the girls and select one, you went to a large window which was actually one-way glass. We could see through it but on the girl's side it was a mirror. Inside there was a small set of bleachers where some the girls sat. Others were working on their makeup in the mirror. You check your program, select your favorites, then go to the window and make your choice. This was a straight massage parlor. No funny stuff. We had our own girls for that.

I had to get all this done in four days because I had the duty during one day of our stay in Bangkok. My duty day was kind of a laid-back day and I amused myself with a couple of girls in what we called a bumboat. These were small native canoes that come alongside and try to bum and/or sell stuff to ships tied up along the river. These girls actually had products to sell.

One was sixteen, another fourteen. They were selling soft drinks and also had whiskey if you wanted it. The older one was named Maalee. She was a student and spoke fair English.

She lived near the river and she told me all about her family and life in Thailand and how the Buddhist religion worked.

110

She was a beautiful young lady except that one eye had a cloudy cataract partially covering it, probably from birth, or it may have been a scar. I didn't ask, but I think it was something that could be fixed fairly easily in the States. I thought to myself, *maybe it was a good thing because parents in Thailand often sold pretty daughters into prostitution.*

The girls stayed all day and just dove into the river to cool off or to go to the bathroom. We bought some soft drinks from them and I gave them some souvenirs from the States. I gave Maalee my address and I actually got a letter from her with a school yearbook picture.

Well, after another couple of great days with my girl Nittaya, my time in this wonderland was over. I think if we had had enough to start a new life there, Guns and I would have jumped ship and gone over the hill. But no, it was the sailor's life for us and we soldiered on. We returned to the ship and prepared ourselves for whatever new adventures awaited us.

Our return run down the river was probably the fastest the old *Basswood* ever moved. We were going with the tide and the current this time and really zooming along. I think our wakes may have created some problems for the flimsier structures along the shore. Well, we shot out the mouth of the river and set a course for the Philippines.

Our destination was Sangley Point where there was both a Navy Air Station and a Coast Guard Air Detachment. But, of more interest to Guns and I and the rest of our red blooded crew, was Cavite City right outside the front gate of the base. It wasn't Bangkok, but more like a miniature Olongapo.

26 CAVITE CITY AND THEN HOME TO GUAM

On the trip back to the Philippines, I had a visit from the skipper. He had been having gut pains and they were getting worse. I was thinking ulcer, probably from the stress that comes from being the person who is ultimately in charge. The commanding officer of a ship has his other officers, as well as the senior non-commissioned officers to advise him. But, he is the one who makes the decisions and who is responsible for whatever may happen under his command.

I prescribed him the best antacid type remedies I had aboard and gave him some advice about items to limit in his diet. I told him to let me know if he started spitting up blood or having dark, tarry stools. I could not give him anything to help him relax like a tranquilizer while he was in command of the ship. I did recommend that he get checked out at the hospital when we got back to Guam.

There was nothing of note about our trip to Sangley Point, except for some very heavy monsoon rains which we hit, leaving Thailand, in the South China Sea. It came down in sheets that you could not even see through. We had about four or five hours of that before we got past the storm system. Other than that, the seas were relatively mild at three to four feet.

It was early March when we pulled into Sangley Point and tied up outboard of the Coast Guard Cutter Nettle. The Nettle was a small freighter like the one used in the film *Mr. Roberts*. The Nettle was the only gray ship in the Coast Guard and she would shortly be turned over (given) to the Philippines.

The Nettle had been used to provide logistics support for our five LORAN stations in the Philippines. Now, a tenant Coast Guard Air Detachment had been established at the naval air station and they started using HU-16 E Albatross seaplanes to take over the logistic duties. We had also turned over the Cutter Kukui in Honolulu to the Philippines. This was in preparation for ultimately phasing out the Loran "A" stations in the Pacific, and she was no longer needed.

Well, as you can imagine, the whole crew was anxious to get ashore and sample the liberty in Cavite City, none more so than the old gunner's mate. It had been a long, dry spell for all of us while we were working in Vietnam. After we were tied up alongside the Nettle, the deck force had temporarily placed a long heavy plank between the two ships. It ran from our buoy deck to the Nettle's cargo deck. This was to facilitate the quick hook up of water and power to our ship. They would later haul the gangway down from the fantail and put in place with a safety net under it.

Well, Guns was a shitting and a getting and stepping out smartly in tropical dress whites and flat hat. He was waiting for neither man, nor the permanent gang way. I was playing catch up, and had just stuck my head out of the forward port hatch when I saw Guns, who was about half-way across the plank.

I hollered, "Hey Guns, wait up." He swiveled his head to see who was calling him and walked right off that damned plank. I shit you not; it was just like a Road Runner cartoon. One second he was there, the next he was gone. The only thing missing was his empty hat floating in the air.

I was laughing so hard I was crying, as I hollered for help to haul his sorry ass out of the drink. It was only about an eight- or ten-foot drop and he was not hurt, except maybe his pride. When we got him back aboard, the deck force charged up a hose and we washed him off before he could go back into the ship. I don't even want to tell you what can be found in the harbor waters of Third World countries. Use your imagination.

Guns took a shower, put on a new uniform, and we were soon on the beach in Cavite City laughing about the whole thing over a drink. Poor old Guns had to suffer a lot of shit over that little fall during the following days. The crew could not seem to get over ribbing him about his mishap. "God damned liberty hound, couldn't wait for the real gangway."

Well, everyone enjoyed their liberty in Cavite City, drank their fill, got their ashes hauled, and no one got into trouble. And I just knew that fact had to have helped the skipper's ulcer. We were now back underway for Guam. With the exception of the married guys, we were not looking forward to that.

The shitty liberty notwithstanding, there were other evolutions taking place in Guam.

There would be crewmembers leaving, including Guns in April. We would lose our now seasoned ensigns and get a couple of green ones. A new XO was also reporting aboard. All the work in the near future would be close to home around the Mariana Islands of Guam, Saipan, Rota, and Tinian. Saipan was the only one of those with even a remote chance of any kind of sailor's liberty.

The only bright spot for me was a month-long medical research trip scheduled for the end of April. We would be traveling to some very remote atolls and islands in the outer Carolines. No liberty per say, but a chance to see islands and people who have been virtually untouched by

113

modern civilization. This appealed to the intellectual side of my nature. And yes, I had one of those, right alongside of the fun-loving and hell-raising side.

27 GUAM IS STILL NOT GOOD

As we pulled into our dock in Apra Harbor, I saw my forlorn little Corvair convertible, covered in dust and seagull shit with the left rear tire going flat. I decided it had been a dumb move to have it shipped over to Guam. I should have sold it before we left Hawaii. I decided to clean it up, put a For Sale sign on it, and then use it to do a comprehensive exploration of the island. Just to see if we had missed anything, and at the same time advertising that the car was for sale.

The new XO and the two new ensigns were waiting at the dock when we pulled in. The current XO, Mr. Young, had been selected for a master's degree program. So he was being replaced by Lieutenant Max Crohn. The ensigns included a kid with white blonde hair named Kevin Pringle, who was the son and nephew of a pair of Coast Guard admirals. There was no Coast Guard career in Kevin's future.

He had received some kind of a liberal arts degree and then went to Coast Guard OCS rather take a chance on his draft number being called. The other one, Ensign Juan Prada, was just the opposite. He was the first Guamanian to ever graduate from the Coast Guard Academy and he was career material. They were both, however, inexperienced officers with lots to learn.

One of our other personnel changes had been brewing for a long time. The warrant bosun and the chief bosun's mate just could not get along. They were both of Portuguese decent, both born and raised in Hawaii. One was old school and the other new. When their animosity finally erupted into a near fist fight on the buoy deck, the skipper decided one of them had to go.

The warrant, being senior, chose the ship and our current chief traded jobs with an older chief assigned to the Guam buoy depot located near where we tied up the ship. Although the new chief was no ball of fire, he had gray hair and that seemed to solve the problem for our warrant bosun.

One weekend, the Guns and I cleaned up my car, fixed the rear tire, and took a drive around the island. There really wasn't much. There was an ocean-side park clear around on the back side of the island. Later we had a picnic there for the ship's crew and dependents. But other than that, there was really not much unless you were a cockfighting fan. They had a huge cock fighting pit in a covered arena.

Well, one good thing. Our little drive turned up a buyer for my car. A Guamanian kid showed up a few days later to look at the car. He paid me cash for it, right out of his front pocket. That was one worry taken care of.

I really didn't need a car on Guam. I would buy a new one when and if I received orders back to the U S of A.

Well, we had a little time to kill around Guam before Guns got transferred and we left on our next buoy run. We made the best of it that we could, but there was really not much of our kind of liberty on Guam. I did go out for the annual billfishing tournament. The Navy Recreation Department had a couple of seagoing tugs outfitted for deep sea fishing and a few of us checked it out. We caught some wahoo, a couple mahimahi, and one small swordfish.

Then another time, six of us chartered a small plane to fly us over to Saipan where they liked us much better than the Guamanians and liberty was pretty good. Other activities included going out to Anderson Air Force Exchange to buy stuff or hanging around the Merchant Marine Club. Around the middle of April, after Guns left, I was kind of lost. Oh, I had other buddies to hang out with, but they weren't Guns.

We had a buoy run to Saipan scheduled the week after Gunderson left. After that, we were going to be deployed on the medical research trip to Yap and the outer Caroline Islands. The Saipan trip would use up about six or seven days and then back to Guam to get fueled and supplied for the medical trip. That trip would use up the last of April and most of May.

28 THE SAIPAN STORY

I tried to get the skipper to check himself into the medical clinic for his ulcers. He said no because he wanted to give the new XO, Mr. Crohn, a little more experience first. He figured that they would pull him off the ship for surgery. The XO would then be acting CO and the skipper wanted to give Mr. Crohn time to get a handle on the job. The CO promised he would go to the hospital after the Saipan trip. So, we sailed away to go fix buoys on Saipan.

Saipan was an interesting island. We had been on one previous buoy run. We had brought some aviation fuel over as part of a typhoon relief mission. A couple of other guys and I had chartered a plane and flown over one weekend. It was a lot friendlier place than Guam. It had an area of about forty-four square miles, a mountain, nice beaches, and a population of about six thousand five hundred.

It also had the dubious honor of having been the costliest victory in the Pacific Campaign during WWII. The battle was fought between June 15 and July 9, 1944.

Of the 71,000 Americans who fought, 2,949 were KIA and 10,464 were wounded. The Japanese began the battle with 31,000 well dug-in and fortified defenders. Only 921 survived, 5000 of the casualties were due to suicide.

The Japanese had been settling on Saipan for many years. During the war, more than 26,000 Japanese civilians lived there. When it looked as if the battle was lost, Emperor Hirohito radioed the island and told the population that the Americans would do terrible things to them if captured and that they should all commit suicide. Over 22,000 civilians perished, mostly from suicide. More than 1,000 of them jumped from suicide or *banzai* cliffs into the rocky shore below.

Saipan was also known for the largest *banzai* attack of the war. Over 3000 of their soldiers charged and almost overran the American forces. One other notable event took place during the battle of Saipan. Actor Lee Marvin was wounded during the assault on Mount Tapachau with I Company, 24th Marines. He was hit in the buttocks and the wound severed his sciatic nerve. He received a medical discharge as a result. They just don't make actors like that anymore.

Enough history. We arrived at Saipan in the afternoon and liberty was granted. We would be there for two days working local aids to navigation. This was my first liberty in over a year when Guns was not with me or in the vicinity. I was kind of lost without him, just wandering around with a couple of the other guys, seeing the sights.

There was an interesting old church there. I wanted to get some photos. Most of the island infrastructure had been built by the Japanese; roads, airstrips, lighthouses, harbors, and they had all been built to last.

There were only two hotels on the island. One old island-style hotel on the side of the mountain was owned by a retired Navy chief petty officer. The other was newer, a pink stucco building right on the beach. The beach was interesting in that you could still see the turrets and cannons of several American WWII tanks sticking out of the water. They obviously did not make it to the beach during the landing

After wandering for a while, we went to the local cockfights and watched those for a bit. After that, I found a bar where I could get a drink and something to eat. I also met a little island girl while I was there. We had a few drinks together before she suggested that we buy some beer and go to her place. I said okay and she said to wait so she could get her sister. She came back in a few minutes with her sister and, oh shit, Lucky was with the sister.

Of course, hindsight is 20/20. What I should have done was excuse myself, and make up a story that I had to hurry back to the ship. At this point, as often happens, my little head was doing the thinking for my big head. We bought two cases of Kirin Beer. The girls each put one on their head and lead us through the jungle to their little thatched hut. We drank and partied and had a good time. At some point we fell asleep.

The next morning the hot sun beating down on my head through a window opening woke me and one thing flashed in my mind. *Oh shit, we're late.* I woke Lucky and we both went out the window like high hurdlers and hit the ground running. When we got to the road, we flagged down an old man in a WWII Jeep. We paid him our last $5.00 to take us to the harbor. When we arrived, the ship was just a black speck on the horizon. I thought to myself, *I'm fucked and look who I'm with.*

Lucky crawled into the cab of an old truck parked there and slept. This was business as usual for him. I sat on the pier leaning up against a bollard and worried. And I was really pissed at myself. Well, I knew if there was anything good about the situation, it was that the ship was working locally and would be back in to stay for another night. Boy, was I going to catch hell. Shit, I could lose a stripe over this. But, what was worse, if someone got injured working a buoy or had some other kind of an accident, I wasn't there to take care of them.

The ship returned that afternoon and we were put on report by the master at arms. After that, I was taken up to the commanding officer's cabin, where he was looking over my report sheet and shaking his head.

"Jesus Doc, what am I going to do with you? I'm really hesitant to take this to a Captain's Mast and ruin eleven years of good conduct. What the hell were you doing with Lucky?"

"Skipper, there is nothing you could do or say to me that would make me feel any worse than I already do. All I could think about while I was waiting for the ship is what if someone got hurt and I was not there. I think two things happened. Guns is gone and I got hooked up with Lucky purely by chance. I should have excused myself and passed on the girl and returned to the ship right then."

"Well, Doc, you've been an exemplary sailor up to this point and that's the only thing saving your ass. I'm going to let you slide on this, but I want you to know that you've really let me down. When we get back to Guam, they're going to put me in the hospital. Mr. Crohn will be acting CO until I get back on my feet. He is going to need everyone's help."

"So please, get your shit back together and be someone he can depend on."

"Yes sir, thank you sir."

29 TRAVELING BACK IN TIME

We had about a week to go before we departed on, what I considered would be, the trip of a lifetime. No, brawls, no wild drunks, no bar girls. Just a month-long trip to someplace in the world that few have ever been. These islands and people are so far off the beaten path that they have had almost no contact with the modern world.

I really like this kind of stuff. When I was a little kid, I would sit with my grandmother and we would read the National Geographic and wonder about places we would probably never see. By this point in my life, I had seen many of those places. The next would be Yap. I particularly remembered Yap because of my grandmother reading to me about the natives and their big stone money, *rai*.

The acting CO Mr. Crohn was a nice guy and a quick study. He was getting settled in at his new job of commanding the ship in the skipper's absence. We were about the same age and got along pretty well.

I guess he had heard stories in the wardroom about some of my liberty escapades and he liked to tease me about my adventures ashore.

We had a couple new ensigns, but now we also had a seasoned enlisted crew.

Many of the young guys who had come aboard right out of boot camp and reported for duty before we left Hawaii were now third class petty officers. We did not anticipate any problems during our upcoming trip, except maybe finding a couple of the atolls we wanted to visit. At least one of them didn't even appear on our nautical charts.

Getting out of Guam was always a good thing, as far as I was concerned. This was also going to be my last patrol on the ship. The rest of the time I was aboard, we would be working local aids to navigation. I would have more time hanging around Guam than I wanted so, I was more than ready to get underway.

Our first stop was Yap, the largest island in the Yap group of the Caroline Islands. There was a small community there, the island administration, and a regional Peace Corps training center. I don't recall if there was a bar, but I wasn't much interested in drinking on this trip. I was more interested in learning what I could and getting some good pictures.

I got a lucky break once again by being the corpsman. The Senior Researcher was a veterinarian, a commander in the United States Public Health Service. He brought a buddy of his, who was an M.D., along to help. When he found out about my medical training and experience, he asked the CO if he could use me to help collect samples. The ship's yeoman (clerk) also got selected to help record information about the samples we collected.

This meant that we would be able to go ashore on these very remote islands while the rest of the crew would have to remain aboard the ship.

Actually, Yap was a beautiful island in its own right. It had a beautiful deep green lagoon and a small harbor. This is where we started going the other way in time and got our first look at bare-breasted native women and men in loincloths.

One of the complaints made by the Peace Corps women training there was that they could not hang their bras out to dry when they washed them. The Yapese women were curious about them, and they stole them. Not because they wanted to wear them, but because they didn't think the Peace Corps women should. It wasn't natural.

One other thing I noticed on Yap was that everybody, even little kids, chewed betel nut. They sprinkle them with lime salt, wrap them in a leaf, and chew them. Over time, the lime salt destroys the enamel on their teeth. They had to keep chewing because the mild narcotic eased the resulting pain of exposed tooth pulp. And of course, some of our guys had to try it.

I spent the day hiking around the island looking at the different sized *rai* stones. I even got a picture in front of one particularly large one that I remembered seeing in one of my grandmother's National Geographic magazines way back in the 1940s. As far as I could tell, the Yapese are the only ones who quarry and make *rai*. The value comes not only from the size, but from the cost of going to get it and getting it back to Yap.

The stones were quarried on Palau Island, some 250 miles by sea. They traveled by outrigger canoes to quarry the rock and form the *rai* and then transport it back to Yap.

Some of the big ones had to weigh close to a half ton. Lives were almost always lost on these trips. Hence the value, travel + labor + lives = Value. Yep, size mattered.

After my trek out to photograph the *rai*, I came to an open area near the harbor where I saw a crowd of Coasties and natives surrounding a very tall coconut palm tree. One of the native men was naked and he was holding a Coast Guard work uniform over one arm. Everyone was looking up, so I looked up. There was Lucky, showing his ass, literally. He was wearing the native's loincloth and he was about three-quarters of the way up the tree. His pasty legs and white butt cheeks hung out for all to see and he was going up the tree like a monkey, while everyone on the ground cheered. Fucking Lucky strikes again. Well, at least he didn't get in any trouble for this one.

There was one other ship in the harbor, the *Yap Islander*. It was a small inter-island freighter about half the size of our ship. It was a rusty old trade vessel manned by local natives. It traveled around to the remote islands to trade with other natives. They traded for carvings, sea and turtle shells, and on some islands, copra. We were able to get a rough chart showing the location of the first island we wanted to visit. They said it was so small and out of the way that they didn't even get there very often, maybe every three or four years.

The Peace Corps folks were not too much help in terms of useful information. Their mission was to teach sanitation and English. The sanitation part was trying to get the remote islander to shit in outhouses. It was an altogether stupid idea.

The Peace Corps had representatives on the more populated islands, including one of the islands on our list, Woleai, which had a population of about 650 people.

They had shipped cases of toilet paper out to the more remote islands on the *Yap Islander*. We will talk about that later.

30 THE RESEARCH AND OUR PASSAGE TO IFALIK

What was the research about and why the remote islands? The disease was called toxoplasmosis. It's an intracellular protozoan that is transmitted from animal to man, but at the time, they did not know which animal or exactly how it was transmitted. The disease, however, could be transferred from a pregnant mother to the unborn child in the womb and cause birth defects. Toxoplasmosis was endemic in this part of the Pacific. They figured that the remote islands would make a good laboratory. It was someplace where the number of people and animals were limited, as were their contacts with the outside world.

Our mission at the first island was to draw blood or other samples from every living animal and human on the island. The research doctor had devised a way to collect just the right amount of blood. He used small disks made of an absorbent paper. When fully soaked, they would hold the amount of blood needed for testing in his laboratory. These blood samples would be reconstituted with sterile water back at the laboratory, and the various tests would be performed.

On the larger islands, we would collect samples from any species that were not present on the first island.

The first two islands were so small and pristine that only the research team would be going ashore. Allowing the crew ashore and having sixty Coast Guardsmen tramping around would have a devastating effect on the delicate environment found on these remote human sanctuaries. We would spend at least two days at each island plus steaming time there and between islands.

The first island we were stopping at was Ifalik, which we found had a population of 147. This was followed by Eauripik with about 250 people, and then the largest island on our list, Woleai. Ifalik did not show up on our nautical charts. We were using our charts, as well as information provided by locals on Yap, to chart our course through and around the hundreds of small coral atolls between Yap and our destination about 430 miles to the southeast.

As we set sail on this part of our trip, I felt we were actually traveling back into time. In a sense, we were. The seas were quiet and calm. I could imagine that I was on an old wooden square-rigger with Captain Cook on a journey of discovery. It was as if I could hear the creaking of the masts and the sails popping as we beat into the soft island trade winds. The rigging straining made distinct sounds and somewhere there was a knocking noise, perhaps a block and tackle swinging loose with motion of the ship. I could feel the cant of the deck under my feet and could hear the soft "Shisssssss" sound the hull made as it cut through the sea. When I looked up, I saw puffy, white clouds and a lone albatross floating high in the blue sky following along with the ship.

Down on the surface of the sea, there were porpoises jumping and playing in our bow wake. Then, the "steady thrum" of our diesel electric engines brought me back to the present.

I still could not kick the feeling of an earlier time as we passed many small atolls that were like beautiful green emeralds tossed out on a blue surface. They had white sand beaches and tall palm trees and were surrounded by coral reefs which formed blue-green lagoons. The water that radiated out from these atolls was a lighter shade of blue than the lagoons or the deep blue of the surrounding seas. It was a wonderful sight to behold.

When we arrived at Ifilik, it was also a beautiful Island. There were actually two islands on an almost perfectly round coral atoll. The main island was 1.4 square miles in area. It looked to be about the size of two football fields from end to end. There was one smaller, uninhabited island located perpendicular to the main island, just across the narrow entry into a beautiful deep lagoon.

The one break in the coral reef was not big enough for the ship to pass through into the lagoon. The skipper anchored outside the reef and the research party, including yours truly, went ashore in one of our 26' small boats. Even then, as I looked back at our shirtless coxwain with the sun at his back and the boat's tiller under his arm, I couldn't kick the feeling that we were early explorers. It seemed that I could almost hear the sound of oars beating the water as our surfboat made its way to the shore.

The small boat slid up on the beach at one end of the island and cut its engine. As we stepped out onto the sands of another time, I had this hollow feeling of anticipation in my gut and a kind of electric excitement surrounded me as a chill ran up my spine.

This was brand new territory for all of us. The head of the expedition had done a lot of research on these people. He had been educating me all the way out from Guam. I thought it was very interesting and I was really looking forward to meeting these people from an earlier time.

31 IFALIK

The first thing I noticed was the quiet. All I could hear was the gentle lapping of the ocean as it slid softly onto the white sand beach. The palm trees were very tall, I would guess, close to a hundred feet. On the island of Oahu they call them royal palms and they had some of the best specimens surrounding the front of the Iolani Palace. At any rate, these trees were regal and there were a lot of them. There were also shorter trees and tropical shrubs beneath the canopy of palm fronds.

As we entered the tropical forest, we noticed a well-used path in the sandy soil and followed it. Everything in the forest seemed un-naturally neat and clean, as if the place had been cleaned up for our arrival. The gloom of the interior was broken up by shafts of sunlight coming through the jungle canopy. It was just a short walk to a small village in the center of the island. Here we encountered our first islanders. I don't know exactly how, but it seems like they were expecting us.

I know that the trip was months in the planning. The doctor had been communicating with people in the Trust Territories and on Yap in preparation. I guess the word had filtered out to this far flung little atoll somehow.

As we entered the open space in the center of the village, to the left was a large Long House which we later found out was the Men's House where single men lived. To the right was a beach with several outrigger canoes pulled up on it. To the right of that, and a little farther inland, was a canoe house with a huge canoe inside of it. Think *Kon-Tiki*. This we found out was used to evacuate the island for some reason, a tidal wave maybe, or to make trading trips to other nearby islands. I guess the whole village would fit in it. Outside, in front of the boat house, was a gathering spot for the men to drink *tuba* (coconut liquor) and tell stories at the end of the day.

From the boat house in a semi-circle around the open area were several of their thatched palm dwellings where the families lived. Off by itself was another larger hut. I guess you could call it the blood hut. This is where women had to live during their monthly period. They were not allowed to participate in any social functions during that time. The village girls also went here to live for six months after the start of their menstruation. Here, the older women schooled them in the facts of life and the responsibilities that came with being adult women.

These folks had a village chief and two sub-chiefs. The people, for lack of a better description, still lived by the old "taboo" system and the chiefs made all the important decisions for the villagers. For instance, I noticed three large sea turtles, a delicacy to these people.

They were turned on their backs in the shade and covered with leaves and kept wet. They could live for up to fourteen days like that until the chief decided on an auspicious occasion to have a feast.

It was also taboo for the women to go in the small canoes. And whenever a woman approached or passed near a man, they had to make sure that they kept their heads lower than the man's. This meant that if a man were seated, the woman would have to crawl up to him. I'm sorry ladies, but woman's liberation had not reached these islands.

The people were sitting quietly, either in or in front of these various buildings. The men wore red- or blue-colored loincloths and the women and girls were topless and wore either a grass skirt or a woven fiber skirt depending on their age. The pre-pubescent girls wore the grass skirts and the adult women wore the fiber skirts. The people were Micronesian and were smaller in stature than their Polynesian cousins. This is probably because they were mixed with early migrants from the Philippines or Malay Archipelago.

The men were maybe 5'5" to 5'8" with muscular upper bodies, probably from diving for fish, paddling canoes, and climbing palm trees. The women had tight, curly-black hair and tended to become chubby in adulthood after childbirth. The women also didn't do much in the way of physical activity. They seemed to do everything from a sitting position, like cooking meals. With these people, the women sat and sang or chanted. The men did the dancing. In fact, singing and dancing is how they preserved much of their history, as it was passed down from generation to generation.

As we entered the village, an old, white-haired man in a red loincloth and a teenage boy in a blue loincloth approached us. This was the high chief and the boy would translate. He had gone to a Catholic Mission school on Ulithi, an island near Yap, and could speak some English.

He was able to convey to the chief and people what it was we needed from them.

The research doctor handed the chief a carton of cigarettes, which he was glad to receive. It seems no matter how primitive the people, our vices always seem to find them. Although, I imagine that cigarettes were hard to come by on these very remote islands. The chief was the only one I saw smoking while we were there.

I noticed the boy looking at my watch. It was just a Timex. I took it off and gave it to him. He probably just admired it as a piece of jewelry, because these people certainly had no need to know what time it was. Nature told them everything about time they needed to know.

After the formalities were over, the women got all giggly and ran up and put flowers in our hair. Making sure, of course, their heads were lower than ours. One of the men kept scooting up palm trees and bringing coconuts down for us to drink. If you finished one, he would fetch you another. When I figured this out, I just sipped my coconut water. Other of the men took the outriggers out to the ship to trade with our guys, and dance for them on the buoy deck. The women had to stay on the island because, as I mentioned before, they could not ride in the small canoes.

Eventually, we got them all lined up so we could take blood samples from them using a lancet and doing a finger stick.

All in all, we took blood samples from 147 people, 1 cat, 6 pigs, and a bunch of chickens. We also made kill jars and captured the two species of day-biting mosquitoes present on the island. It took us two days to complete our sampling.

After the day's work, we took a dip in the lagoon. We were then entertained with the women's singing and chanting, and the men dancing the stick-dance which depicted combat from some point back in their history when this was a warrior island. It was interesting to note that some of the chants the women did had German words and numbers in them. The Spanish discovered these islands, as I've said before, but at some point they were sold to the Germans who held them until the end of the First World War. The fact that these islands were allowed to remain primitive was because of their size, their remote location, and the fact that they had nothing that the outside world could exploit for profit.

The only modern implement to be found were a few iron pots, some steel knifes and machetes, the cloth for loincloths, and a few boards in a couple of their larger buildings. Everything else was made by hand with materials found on their islands or washed up on the shore. The large canoe in the boat house was totally handmade, including sails. The colors and dyes used were made from native plants. They were very good carvers. They used this skill, as well as the unusual and large seashells to be found in and around their waters, to trade with the *Yap Islander* on those years that she stopped at their island. I was able to get a couple of nice carvings and a canoe paddle as well as helmet and trumpet conch shells.

The research team slept in the men's house during the night we stayed on the island.

As I was laying there by the door that night, one of the natives just outside, was struggling with something in his hands. When I looked, I found it was a can of soda. He must have traded for it while on the ship. He could not figure out how to open the pull tab. I was just about to help him when he became impatient, whipped out his machete, and opened it the same way he would a coconut. The can of carbonated soda exploded and covered him with whatever was in the can. He wandered off mumbling, probably some native expletives.

The next day when I returned to the ship, I was told how the natives were fascinated by cold. We would hand one of them a cold can of soda right out of the cooler. They would handle it as you and I would have if we were handed a hot potato right out of the oven. And ice, from the ice machine. They, of course, had never seen ice.

Well, it had been a wonderful visit. I was encouraged to learn that they had put to good use the toilet paper that the Peace Corps had shipped out to them. The native girls had torn the toilet paper sections apart and used them to create little macramé flowers. They used these to make small leis to decorate their hair. From more than a couple of feet away, you could not tell that they were not real flowers.

So, how did these uncivilized people relieve themselves? They walked waist deep into the ocean in an area where they were very familiar with the tides and currents. Then they did their business. In just minutes, the waste was far out to sea where it became just another biodegradable substance. These few people, in a very large surrounding ocean, did not pollute anything. On the other hand, they knew instinctively that digging outhouses on islands that were only about ten feet above sea level, like the Peace Corps wanted them to do, would contaminate their drinking water.

The drinking water consisted of rainwater caught and stored in stone-lined cisterns in the ground.

So, as we sailed away, I was thinking these people were not so primitive after all. They were happy as children. They had everything that they needed for a good life and very few people from the outside world ever bothered them. And guess what, the M.D. with us went around and did some cursory medical exams on these people and found that nobody was sick. He also told me that statistically, the death at birth rate for people in this part of the world, who were born in dirt-floor thatched huts, was exactly that of the USA with all our modern medical miracles.

We were on our way to Eauripik and had just got up to our cruising speed of 11 knots. I was out on the fantail, as usual, with a cup of coffee in my hand. I heard the loud trumpet of a conch shell. As I looked around, I saw the big outrigger from Ifalik passing us to starboard. She had the wind in her sails and had to be traveling at about

20 knots. They were on their way to let the folks on Eauripik know that we were coming. Primitive people, indeed. Out here, we were the primitives.

32 EAURIPIK, WOLEAI, AND BACK TO GUAM

Eauripik was more of the same, just a little bigger. There were enough coconut palms on Eauripik to harvest some of the coconuts, dry them, and sell them as copra. Copra, at one time, was known as white gold. It is used in many food products, as well as cosmetics. After the coconuts were harvested, they were split and dried in copra sheds. These were thatched huts with raised floors and were built to let the air filter in through all sides to enhance the drying process.

The copra did provide us with one more species to sample, copra rats. We trapped and killed a few and the doctor opened their chests so adequate blood samples could be obtained directly from their hearts. After we had sufficient samples of everything the doctor needed for his studies, we departed for our last stop, Woleai.

Woleai would be a little different. It was larger with a population of about 650 people, and it actually had a Peace Corps volunteer stationed on the island.

Since the researchers were able to get what they needed from the first two islands, and these people had a little more exposure with the outside world, this was just going to be a visit and the crew was being allowed ashore. The crew was also told if anyone laid a hand on one of these island girls or any of the natives for that matter, that they would be flogged and then keelhauled.

As we were dropping anchor, we saw a native outrigger approaching the ship. There appeared to be a white man among the people in the canoe, but the only way you could tell was by his blond hair and the Nikon camera hanging around his neck. He was wearing a native loincloth and was very, very tan. When he got aboard, we noticed that his ears were pierced with bamboo plugs and he had tattoos of porpoises down both of his legs like some of the natives.

The Peace Corps guy was taken to the wardroom where they noticed he had a thousand-yard stare and found out that he was nearing the end of his two-year tour. When they noticed him looking at a bowl of fresh fruit on the wardroom table, they asked him if he would like some. He took an apple. He was asked if he would like some fruit to take back with him.

He thought for a couple of minutes and then said, "Naw, too much bother, this apple's fine."

Then, he was asked if he would like to take a nice warm, fresh water shower. Again, after thinking about it he responded, "Naw, I'll just jump in the lagoon when I get back."

130

When asked where his clothes were, he said that most of them had rotted and besides, what he was wearing was a lot more practical and comfortable in this environment.

His duties on the island were to teach the natives English and sanitation.

When asked how that was going, he said some of the youngsters and teens had picked up English pretty well. The sanitation, not so much. When the skipper found out that he had been a Purdue football star, he told the gentleman that we had the college playoffs on film. The skipper said they could bring the projector and a portable generator ashore and show them. The skipper said they could tack a big piece of canvas between a couple of palm trees for a screen. Since Purdue was in the playoffs, he thought it would be a good idea. He also he said the natives had never seen a movie nor a football game.

When we got ashore, the whole community turned out and seemed excited and happy to see us. I think their island was the prettiest of the bunch. All the open space was covered with some kind of green ground cover almost like a lawn. There were some more substantial dwellings here, and even a couple of white picket fences. I could tell right away which hut belonged to the Peace Corps guy. It had a pile of concrete outhouse platforms in front of it with weeds growing up through them.

And indeed, the young folks were anxious to try out their English on us. I approached one extremely lovely teenage girl. I told her I thought she was beautiful and asked if I could take her picture. She said that I should see her twin sister. Then, she asked me if I wanted to go play on the reef that night. I was not sure what that meant, but I politely turned her down. I sure as hell did not want to be keelhauled.

The football movies were a gas. The islanders really loved them, as did the Peace Corps worker. All were hollering and screaming and cheering.

When the film was over, a bunch of the native guys grabbed a coconut, and using it as a football, started up their own impromptu football game. The way they were hitting and tackling each other, I was sure someone would be hurt, but it didn't happen. They're pretty tough people.

After our visit, it was back to the ship and off to our home port on Guam. In a way, I was saddened as we left these happy people and their islands. I guess I'm a romantic at heart, but I was wishing that the missionaries and the Peace Corps could leave these simple islanders alone. I think our planet needs places where there are still some people living happily, untouched by modern civilization. Intellectually, I knew this would never happen. As long as there is one uncivilized person left, there will always be a missionary trying to bring him into the fold.

After arriving back on Guam, the first few months were going to be spent doing some local work and providing much needed maintenance to the ship, not to mention a rest for the crew. It had been a busy year. We were all ready for some down time and the married guys needed time with their families.

I needed the time as well, because I had lots of things to get done before I transferred in the middle of October. I had been right. I was not getting a back-to-back tour. My request for assignment to the CGC *Blackhaw* in the Philippines had been shot down. So, the adventure was over, at least for now. As I prepared to leave, I promised myself that one day I would be back.

EPILOGUE

My orders had me going back to the Base Alameda dispensary in the San Francisco Bay Area in California. I needed to be sure that my medical department on the ship was in good shape for whomever relieved me. I also needed to prepare for my forthcoming urban lifestyle. If I wanted to continue my Coast Guard career, it was also time for me to ship over.

There was a special shipping over bonus going on for certain rates. Corpsman was one of them. To make sure that I got in on it, I shipped over three months early. I received my regular $2,000.00 bonus plus a $6,000.00 variable reenlistment bonus for a total of $8,000.00, which was a lot of money in 1968.

The first thing I did when I got the bonus was go to the Air Force Exchange and order a brand new 1969 Corvette, T-Top Roadster. Being in a duty-free, no tax area, I paid less than $5,000.00 cash. It would be delivered to a San Francisco dealership about a month after I arrived in California.

Other than that, we had one last ship's party before the majority of us from the long deployment rotated out. I sure wished Guns could have been there. Finally, it was time for me to go, 15 October 1968. I was a sad puppy as I went down the gangway of the old girl because I knew she still had a few adventures left in her. I threw my seabag in, then climbed into the transport van over to Anderson Air Force Base for the flight back to the States.

I really missed old Guns, and thought of him on the way over to Anderson. I hoped that he was enjoying his new ship. If I had to guess, I would say that he was probably in some Boston waterfront sailor bar, drinking Brave Bulls, playing his concertina, and telling sea stories about us and our days aboard the *Basswood*.

With the Corvette and the extra bonus cash, I was going to put the best face I could on my return to CONUS. I would get some new clothes and an apartment on the beach in Alameda and check out the action. If Guns had been around, he would have told me that it was not going to work. And it didn't. In retrospect, I should have purchased an old beat-up VW van with flowers and peace symbols painted all over it. Then dressed myself in some ragged bell bottoms, some granny glasses, and a long haired wig. Those were the guys who were getting all the action. Yours truly, who grew up John Wayne straight, was having to make do with forty-something, over the hill bar maids.

133

Well, that was not going to cut it for me. I put in for orders to go back overseas. I made a real pest of myself until I got my way.

Nine months later, the Corvette was sold to some other young guy who thought that was the answer. Shortly after that, I found myself in the Philippine jungle on a remote fifteen-man LORAN station located on the South China Sea about 500 miles from Vietnam and around eighty miles from the island of Borneo. I would remain there for two years and experience many new adventures, but that my friends, is another story if I live long enough to write it.

The *Basswood* was de-commissioned in 1998 and sold. She had given fifty-five years of service to her country and also provided a home, an occupation, and a source of adventure to three generations of young Coast Guardsmen. After a decade and a half of abuse by her new owners, she was scrapped. Now the *Basswood* lives on only in the collective memories of those of us who sailed in her during her glory days. When the last of us are gone, she will also be no more.

Late at night, in the quiet of my writing room, as I sit in front of my computer, I can sometimes bring her back. I'll stretch my cramped muscles, lean back, close my eyes, and I'm aboard the *Basswood* again. I can feel the roll of her decks and the vibrations from her powerful diesel electric engines under my feet. Sea spray carried by an errant breeze, caresses my skin. I can smell the salt air, the stack gas, and the noon-meal cooking down in the galley. As I look forward towards the horizon, I can see the endless blue where the sky meets the sea. I take in a deep breath through once-strong lungs and the adventures return. I no longer feel the aches and pains of my arthritic old bones. For a moment or two I am young again, young again, young again.

Semper Paratus.

GLOSSARY

aft	Towards the rear of the ship
air castle	A covered but open air space on a ship's main deck
APC	Aspirin with caffeine
AWOL	Absent without leave
BDU	Battle dress uniform
benjo	Open air sewer in Japanese language
billet	A job description of duties on a ship
bollard	Mooring post on a pier
bosun	A shortened term for the boatswain's mate
bosun rating	Boatswain's mate is the primary deck rate on a ship
brass	A collective term for military officers
Brave Bull	A tequila-based cocktail mixed with coffee liqueur
bridge	Where a ship is navigated from
brow	Gangway to board ship
bulkhead	Wall
buoy deck	The forward main deck on a buoy tender where buoys are repaired
chief	A chief petty officer (a senior Non-commissioned officer)
Cinderella liberty	Have to be back aboard the ship by midnight
CO	Commanding Officer
Cobra gun ship	A combat helicopter
compartment	A room on a ship
concertina	A small accordion
coxwain	Pilot of a ship's small boat
CS2	Commissary man second class, a cook
deck	Nautical term for floor
didi	To run away, from the Vietnamese '*didi mau len*'
DMZ	Demilitarized Zone
dog faces	Infantry soldiers
dojo	Martial arts training studio in Japanese language
EM Club	Enlisted Men's Club (Bar)
enfilade	Military formation in relation to enemy fire
fantail	Main deck on stern of ship
flying bridge	Lookout bridge above the navigation bridge
fore	Anything forward on a ship, opposite to aft

forecastle	Upper deck forward on ship
galley	Kitchen on a ship
Green Machine	Slang for Marine Corps
grommet	A reinforced hole on a canvas or sail and slang for sphincter muscle or rectum
grunts	Term for ground soldiers or Marines
gunwale	Upper side rail on a ship or boat
Habushu or *habu*	Snake in Japanese language
*haol*e	White person in Hawaiian language
hash marks	Service stripes on uniform sleeve
head	Bathroom
hit the beach	Go on liberty or shore leave
honcho	Person in charge in Japanese language
hooch	A native hut in Vietnam
Hooligan Navy	Derogatory term for Coast Guard
jarheads	A term for Marines due to their high and tight haircuts
John Wayne can opener	A World War II G.I. can opener
JOOD	Junior officer of the deck
keelhaul	Historical: A form of punishment at by dragging the offender through the water under the keel of a ship, either across the width or from bow to stern. Modern: Punish or reprimand severely.
khlong	Canal or tributary in Thai language
Kung Fu	Martial art of China
ladder	Any steps or stairs on a ship
liberty	Shore leave for sailors
LORAN	Long range aid to navigation (a radio beam)
MEDIVAC	Medical evacuation
M 79	A grenade launcher
Muay Thai	Martial art of Thailand
NCO	Non-commissioned officer
OCS	Officer Candidate School
OOD	Officer of the deck
open gangway	Can go on liberty anytime
ordnance	Weaponry, munitions, explosives

overhead	The ceiling
paalam	Good bye in Philippine (Tagalong) language
PBR	Patrol Boat, River
pollywogs	Those who have not been initiated
port	Left side of ship
pumping bilges	Slang for urinating
quarter deck	Portion of deck where OOD station and gangway are located
rack	Bunk or bed
rain locker	Shower
R&R	Rest and recreation or recuperation
RECON	Reconnaissance, spy on enemy position
RPG	Rocket Propelled Grenade
RVN	Republic of Vietnam
sapper	Viet Cong specializing in sneak attacks
scuttlebutt	Gossip
SEALS	Sea Air and Land Navy commandos
sea swells	Waves at sea
Semper Paratus	Coast Guard Motto (Always Prepared/Always Ready)
sensei	Martial arts instructor in Japanese language
shitfaced	Drunk
sick bay	Shipboard clinic
skivvies	Underwear
squids	Derogatory slang for Navy sailors
stanchion	A support pole on a ship
starboard	Right side of ship
stroking it into socks	Term for masturbation into one's socks
tominagi	A sacrifice move in judo in Japanese language
tuk tuk	Three-wheeled motorized rickshaw in Thai language
ulua	Tuna fish
wardroom	Officer's quarters
WESTPAC	Western Pacific Patrol
XO	Executive Officer, second in command on ship
zoo	Low ranking enlisted quarters

ABOUT THE AUTHOR

Charles D. Williams was born in Sacramento, California. In 1957, at the age of seventeen, he enlisted in the U.S. Coast Guard. When he retired in 1984, he was a chief warrant officer. During his twenty-seven year career, Williams served on four ships and visited many exotic ports of call. These included five Asian nations and many islands in the Pacific. He served in Vietnam in 1967 and on a remote Coast Guard long range aids to navigation station on Palawan Island in the Philippines from 1969 to 1971. Williams has been to all fifty U.S. States and has lived in seven of them including Alaska and Hawaii. He now makes his home in Las Vegas, Nevada. "Realm of the Golden Dragon" is his second book.

Made in the USA
San Bernardino, CA
07 April 2016